D0345191

Better to Wish

Family Tree

Better to Wish

The First Generation

ANN M. MARTIN

Scholastic Press / New York

Library of Congress Cataloging-in-Publication Data

Martin, Ann M., 1955–
Better to wish / Ann M. Martin. — 1st ed.
p. cm. — (Family tree ; bk. 1)
Summary: In 1930 Abby Nichols is an eight-year-old girl growing up in Maine, but as
the Depression deepens, and her mother dies, the responsibility of taking care of her
family falls to her, and she has to put her dreams of going to college and becoming a
writer on hold.
ISBN 978-0-545-35942-9 (jacketed hardcover) 1. Families — Maine — Juvenile fiction.
2. Depressions — 1929 — Juvenile fiction. 3. Maine — History — 20th century —
Juvenile fiction. [1. Family life — Maine — Fiction. 2. Depressions — 1929 — Fiction.
3. Maine — History — 20th century — Fiction.] I. Title.
PZ7.M3567585Bf 2013
813.54 — dc23
2012047940

10 9 8 7 6 5 4 3 2 1   13 14 15 16 17

Printed in the U.S.A.   23
First edition, May 2013

The text type was set in Baskerville MT.
Book design by Elizabeth B. Parisi

In memory of my grandmothers,
Adele Read Martin and
Gertrude Palmer Matthews

Prologue

When I was eight years old, an hour could seem like a week and a summer could seem like an eternity. But Mama would say to Rose and me, "Time is flying."

When I was eight, what I wanted to be was ten. A two-number age. When I was ten, I wanted to be twelve. When I was twelve, I wanted to be sixteen. I wanted to be an adult, I wanted to drive a car, I wanted to have a job, I wanted to be independent, I wanted to be a mother.

The years rolled by and eventually I realized that they were rolling faster and faster, and that Mama had been right after all. Time was flying.

I've gotten a lot of things I wished for — children, grandchildren, great-grandchildren. And I've experienced a few things I wouldn't wish on anybody. Pop once said it's a good thing we don't know what's around the corner. I didn't understand what he meant then, but I do now. It's better to wish than to know.

When you have the pleasure of being one hundred years old, when your mind is clear and sharp and you can revisit an afternoon that's ninety-five years past as easily as you can visit yesterday afternoon, then you can piece together the kaleidoscope bits of your life. But like a kaleidoscope, the picture is different every time. Fred is there and then he's gone and then he appears again. Zander swirls into focus slowly and disappears with a great swoop that is unexpected, even now. And Mama and Sarah and Adele, they come and go. Love, too. And money. It's crass, but you can't forget about the money, although it means more to some than to others.

Generation following generation, the little ones who didn't make it, the grown ones who stuck around longer than maybe they should have been allowed. And the secrets. The things hidden and the things unsaid that sometimes cause more trouble and more grief as the years pile up, more than the things brought out into the sunshine for all to see.

But even secrets have their place.

Sitting by the window now, in the shadow of a chestnut tree, longing for a view from a different window in a different time, I dig through my memories and choose one from Lewisport, my first home.

Chapter 1

The night of August 13th was going to be one of the best of the whole summer. Abby Nichols knew it, her sister Rose knew it, every kid up and down their sandy lane knew it. It was just an ordinary weekday in tiny Lewisport, Maine, not a holiday, but by the time darkness fell and the fireflies were blinking, the field across from the Methodist church would be ablaze with lanterns. Nearly everyone in town would be turning out to eat candy apples, win Kewpie dolls at the arcade, and gawk at the posters by the entrance to the side-show. The signs announcing the traveling fair — ONE NIGHT ONLY! — had promised a two-headed snake, and Abby did not intend to miss out on that.

Abby thought about the snake, which she felt sorry for but wanted to see anyway, and about the bearded lady and the fat lady and crab man, who supposedly had crab claws instead of hands. She had only a dime to spend at the fair, and a nickel of that would go toward the sideshow. Maybe her father would relent and give her and Rose an extra dime each, but money had always been tight in the Nichols household, and was even tighter now that the Great Depression had fallen over the country, so extra dimes seemed unlikely.

Abby turned on her side, propped her chin in her hand, and looked out the open bedroom window. In the gray dawn she could see the sand on the other side of Blue Harbor Lane and, beyond that, the dark expanse of the ocean. She heard waves rolling in and saw the shapes of gulls wheeling low over the water. The damp salt air was inside, outside, everywhere, making the bedsheets nearly as wet and heavy as sails.

"Abby?" Rose whispered from her side of the bed. "What's the first thing you're going to do tonight?"

Abby rolled over again and faced her little sister. "Go to the sideshow."

"Really? You're going to spend a whole nickel right away?"

"Don't you want to see the sideshow?"

"Yes, but . . . Abby, now don't tell."

Abby sighed. "Don't make me promise not to tell something." She looked sternly at her little sister. "Please, Rose."

"But I have a plan. And if we tell it, it won't come true."

"Then don't tell me. Keep it a secret."

Rose made a face at Abby and said, "Okay-ay. If you don't want to know my plan."

The room lightened, and the white curtains that Abby's mother had made shifted in the breeze. Abby sat up, swung her legs over the edge of the bed, and, resting her arms on the windowsill, peered down at the road below.

"There's Orrin," she said.

"Got his bucket?" asked Rose.

"He's always got his bucket." Abby leaned out the window. "Orrin!" she called softly. "Orrin!"

Orrin Umhay, an old cap of his father's on his head and a hankie trailing out of one back pocket, grinned up at Abby from the quiet lane. Setting down his empty bucket, he asked, "Want to come with me?"

"Blueberries or clams?" asked Abby.

"Blueberries."

Abby looked over her shoulder at Rose. "Want to go pick blueberries with Orrin?"

Rose stretched her skinny six-year-old legs. "Yes."

"We'll be right down," Abby whispered as loudly as she dared, and she pulled her head back inside.

Rose was already wriggling into her gingham dress, the blue one that Mama had made Abby two years earlier for her sixth birthday.

"Dungarees," said Abby, and pulled the dress off Rose's head. "You'll get all scratched up if you wear a dress for blueberry picking. Hang that up. You can wear it later."

"You don't know everything," muttered Rose, but she put on her dungarees.

"Pop's up," Abby said a few minutes later. She was listening cautiously at the door. "We can stop whispering. I hear him downstairs."

"Maybe he won't let us go."

Abby considered this. "Don't say we're going with Orrin. Just tell him we're going blueberry picking." She brightened. "If he asks, tell him we're picking them as a surprise for Mama."

"All right. But where's Orrin?"

"Gone ahead. Pop won't see him."

Abby and Rose slipped out of their room, the only one on the second floor, and crept to the bottom of the stairs. Luther, their pop, had built the house with his own hands while he was courting Nell, their mama. Pop was the best carpenter in Lewisport, maybe in Barnegat Point, too. Abby had heard people say that many times, and she was proud of her father.

"Where are you girls off to so early?" asked Pop from his place at the kitchen table.

"Blueberry picking," said Rose.

And Abby said, glaring at her sister, "*May* we go blueberry picking?"

Pop glanced through the window. "Isn't even light out yet."

"It's almost," said Rose. "Please?"

"Let them go," spoke up Mama. She turned from the stove and set a plate of eggs in front of Pop.

Pop was always up early. "Early bird catches the worm," he liked to say. "Times may be hard, but there's no excuse for a healthy man not to be holding down a job."

And Mama was usually up early, too, to make sure Pop got a good breakfast in him before he went off to whatever carpentry job he had found. If Mama wasn't up early, it was because she was having one of her bad days, her mind stuck thinking of the two rosebushes and what they meant.

Abby and Rose scuttled out the door before Pop could disagree with Mama, and they caught up with Orrin, who was waiting at the edge of the woods near the spot where Blue Harbor Lane abruptly ended at a rocky beach.

"Hey," said Abby.

"Hey," said Orrin.

Abby had known Orrin since they were five, but she had fallen in love with him three months earlier, toward the end of second grade. She couldn't tell him, though. Some thoughts were better left secret.

"How much money have you got for the fair?" asked Rose as they tramped along the path toward the best blueberry bushes. Abby kicked her ankle, but it was too late.

"Not saying," Orrin replied, and then Abby knew for sure that Orrin didn't have any money at all.

Abby felt like hurting Rose, or at least making her feel as awkward as Orrin looked. "Why don't you tell us your plan for tonight at the fair?" she asked her sister.

"What plan?" said Orrin with interest.

"I said it was a secret!" cried Rose.

"But I thought you wanted me to guess."

"Oh, I'll just tell you anyway." Rose stopped and plucked a blueberry from a scrubby bush and dropped it into the bucket she and Abby were sharing. "I'm going to win a tea set at the ring toss game. I know there'll be a tea set there. If I toss very, very carefully, I bet I can win one with five turns. And if I can't, then I'm going to use my other five cents for five more turns instead of going to the sideshow. But I'm going to get a tea set tonight."

"Good luck," said Orrin, and Abby could tell that he meant it.

The sun grew stronger and the day grew hot. When Abby and Rose got home and gave Mama the bucket of berries, she fed them breakfast and then scatted them up the wooden staircase to change out of their dungarees and into dresses. Mama was good with a sewing machine, and Abby's dresses were handmade, which was nice, but her friend Sarah Moreside sometimes got to go to the dress shop in Barnegat Point and pick out a store-bought dress.

Downstairs, the front door banged and Abby heard Sarah say, "Can Abby come out?"

"Abby!" called Mama. "Sarah's here."

Abby buttoned the last button on her dress, grabbed her red socks, and hurried downstairs with Rose at her heels.

"You go play with Emily," Abby said over her shoulder.

"Oh, let her play with us," said Sarah. "It's okay. Look — new paper dolls. Gran sent them for my birthday. We can all cut out her dresses."

Abby gaped at the flawless pages of outfits for a chubby girl named Little Judy, who at the moment was wearing only frilly underwear. Sarah's offer was very generous, considering that Rose was still hopeless with scissors.

Abby and Sarah and Rose sat on Sarah's front stoop in the warm sun and painstakingly clipped out Little Judy's traveling suit and seaside outfit and lavish lavender Christmas dress and her many, many "School Daze" dresses.

"Imagine having this many clothes," said Rose, concentrating furiously on her scissors, wisps of hair escaping from her braids. "Little Judy must be rich."

"No one's rich these days," said Sarah.

Abby glanced up from the page of Little Judy's complicated traveling suit. "President Hoover must be rich."

"Girls! Come inside, please," called Mama from three doors away.

"We'll meet you back here later," Abby said to Sarah, jumping to her feet.

At home, Mama insisted that Rose and Abby change into fresh dresses and fresh socks and eat soup even though the soup was hotter than the day. "And you need a rest," she said to Rose, who protested until Mama reminded her that she would be up late that night at the fair.

Abby trailed back out of her house. Farther down Blue Harbor Lane, she could see three girls jumping rope, and Orrin and his brother trying to ride a little cart they had built themselves using boards and old wheels from a wagon. Sarah wasn't on her stoop yet, so Abby wandered around behind her own house and stood on the sandy ground and looked at the two rosebushes that Pop had planted, one in 1927 and one in 1928, each time one of Mama's babies hadn't lasted long enough to be born proper. On the babies' head-stones in the graveyard at the church were their names: Millicent Pryor Nichols and Luther Randolph Nichols Jr. But the bushes were just plain bushes without any kind of markers. And they made Mama sad. Sometimes Abby wished they hadn't been planted in the yard where Mama could see them every day.

Sarah called to Abby then, and they worked on Little Judy's outfits for a while longer. Then Rose came outside after her nap and a gang of Blue Harbor Lane children played a noisy game of kick-the-can. Finally the girls split off from the boys to take turns jumping rope, and before Abby knew it, Mama was calling her and Rose inside again. It was time to get ready for the fair.

The people of Lewisport walked to the Methodist church after supper, the children scrubbed and shining, the adults tired but hopeful, pockets jingling with pennies and nickels and dimes. Abby and Rose were wearing their third dresses of the day, and their dimes were tucked into the change purses that they wore on chains around their necks.

"Remember not to say about my plan," Rose whispered to Abby. "It's a secret. If you say anything, you'll jinx it."

The lights of the fair blinked in front of them.

"Lanterns!" said Abby under her breath. "It's beautiful! Remember last year?" She turned to Mama and Pop. Last year there had been a small Ferris wheel and Abby had ridden it so many times she had run out of money. That was why she planned to go to the sideshow first this year, before anything else. "Look, there are Sarah and Emily and Francis and Douglas. Can we walk around with them?"

"Stay together," said Pop.

"Abby, keep an eye on your sister," added Mama.

Abby took Rose by the hand and they ran to their friends. Everyone wanted to see the two-headed snake, except for Rose, who wanted to start winning her tea set.

"Five against one. We win," said Douglas, glaring at Rose and jamming his hands in his pockets.

"We'll go to the arcade right after the sideshow," Abby promised her sister.

"Well, I'm not going in. I'm not spending half my money."

Abby was getting very tired of Rose's stubbornness, but once Rose made up her mind, she was hard to budge. In the end, Abby and Sarah waited with Rose while the others went inside, and then they switched off. Rose resolutely refused to use up half her dime, even when Abby ran out of the wooden trailer, crying, "Rose! It really is a two-headed snake! Two heads, four eyes. And there's a man with claws for hands, just like the signs say!"

But Rose would not give up on her tea set plan. She ignored Abby. "The ar*cade*, the ar*cade*!" she said, pulling her sister's hand. She led the way along the rows of games, past the flashing lights and ringing bells and the *pop-pop* of air guns to the tamer ring toss booth, with its board of prizes at the back.

Rose studied the board. At last she pointed and said, "Look. A china tea set. That's what I want."

Abby looked at the tiny china cups and plates and saucers, packed into a fancy wooden box. "But, Rose," she whispered, "you have to get the ring over the exact middle pop bottle to win that. It's almost impossible."

Rose set her jaw. "I can do it." She handed her dime to the skinny man in a striped shirt who was holding a handful of small wooden rings. "Five, please, mister," she said.

Abby and Sarah watched as Rose, frowning, carefully tossed her rings, one after the other, onto the grid of pop bottles. Most of them fell between the cracks. One landed to the side, missing the bottles altogether. Rose used her remaining five cents to buy five more tries. When she reached for the tenth ring, Abby said to her, "Here," and held out her nickel, but Rose shook her head. "I have to do it with my own money."

She squinted one eye shut and carefully tossed out the last ring. It bounced off the edge of a bottle and landed on the ground.

"*Oh!* So sorry, little lady," said the man in the striped shirt. "Here. A consolation prize." He reached for a balloon, which he fastened to a stick before giving it to Rose.

Rose would not cry. She walked ahead of Abby and Sarah down the midway, the balloon bouncing at her side, until Abby saw a man selling ice cream, and bought one for herself and one for her sister.

Their money was gone. But the carnival blinked and pinged and flashed around them, and the lanterns glowed. Rose held tight to her balloon and Abby thought of the wonders of the sideshow and decided she would write about the two-headed snake on the first day of third grade in Barnegat Point, when her teacher was bound to ask the students about their summer vacations.

Long years later, when Abby was old, very old, she liked to recall this evening. Not because Rose had lost her dime, of course, but because it was pleasant to dwell in this time when losing a dime was the biggest worry she and Rose faced. They hadn't yet learned that it was better not to know what was waiting for them around the corner.

Chapter 2

Abby and Rose lay in their bed, wrapped in each other's arms. There was no wood stove in their little room upstairs, which was all right in the summer. But this was Thanksgiving Day, and even tucked under the bedclothes in her flannel nightgown, Abby shivered.

She felt Rose's breath against her neck, as light as the wing of a moth. "Did you look outside?" Rose whispered.

"It's a blizzard," Abby whispered back. "A real blizzard."

A nor'easter, Pop had said the night before, when Abby and Rose were getting ready for bed. Blowing up the East Coast, just in time for Thanksgiving.

All night long the wind had howled, and just before dawn the snow had begun blowing in great white sheets along Blue Harbor Lane.

"How many inches do you think we have so far?" asked Rose. She was learning about inches and feet in first grade and was proud of her knowledge, especially since Pop was a carpenter. Inches and feet were important to him.

Abby sat up, pulling a quilt around her shoulders, and rested her arms on the windowsill. "I can't tell. The snow is already drifting."

"Give me the covers back. I'm freezing."

"We should get up and help Mama. She has a lot to do today."

"Do you think they'll be able to come?"

Abby could read her sister's mind like the mentalist they'd seen once at a county fair.

"I don't know. Maybe not."

"But we can't have Thanksgiving without Aunt Betty and Uncle Marshall!"

Mama's sister, Aunt Betty, and her husband lived ten miles away in Little Conway with their four children, who were all older than Abby, and who, for that very reason, Abby adored — especially Blaine, who gave her piggyback rides and had taught her to hit a baseball.

"Well, we can't ask them to do anything foolish," said Abby sensibly, sounding a lot like Mama.

"They have to come! They have to! Blaine is going to learn me to burp."

Abby narrowed her eyes at her sister. "*Teach* you to burp. And you'd better not let Mama hear you say that. Or Pop. Come on. Let's go downstairs."

Abby scrambled out of bed and into a wool dress. The dress itched, but at least it was warm. She added wool socks and a sweater. And, because it was Thanksgiving, she brushed her hair fifty times and tied a red ribbon in it.

"Brush *my* hair!" cried Rose.

"No braids today?"

"I want to look just like you."

Abby brushed her sister's hair while Rose counted, and then she tied a pale blue ribbon into a careful bow. When the girls appeared in the kitchen, Mama turned away from the window and said, "Why, you look perfect! My two Thanksgiving chicks."

"But the snow," said Rose.

"Is exciting!" Abby finished up. There was no reason to upset Mama, not on a holiday, and not when Mama was smiling and had called Abby and Rose her Thanksgiving chicks. "Look, Rose." She opened the front door and snow swirled inside.

"Abigail! Close that!" cried Pop. "Right now. You're letting the heat out and I'm not made of money."

Abby closed the door in a hurry. "Sorry, Pop."

Pop tapped his forehead. "When are you going to start thinking? Any fool knows enough not to hold the door open during a blizzard."

"I just wanted to see," said Abby.

"Then look out the window."

Abby sat at the kitchen table with Rose. Pop had already eaten his breakfast and was wandering around the house with his toolbox, searching for things to do, since another of his sayings was "Idle hands are the devil's workshop."

Mama set bowls of oatmeal and glasses of milk in front of Abby and Rose. "Breakfast first, and then you girls can give me a hand with the cooking."

"But, Mama, do you think Aunt Betty and Uncle Marshall are going to come?" asked Rose.

Mama glanced out the kitchen window, where the snow was falling thickly. Abby saw that it had already half buried the two little rosebushes. "I don't know," said Mama, turning back to the stove.

"Maybe we could" — Abby struggled for the proper word — "*postpone* Thanksgiving."

Mama smiled sadly at her. "The turkey is ready to go in the oven, the piecrust is made, and the vegetables can't go for more than a day or two without spoiling. We have to have Thanksgiving today."

"Well, anyway, I still think they're coming," said Rose.

"Finish your oatmeal now," said Mama. "We have a lot to do, storm or no storm. Abby, I want you to peel the potatoes and then help me with the pies. Rose, you can shape the biscuits. Goodness, the icebox is going to be full to overflowing. Thank goodness Joe King came yesterday."

Joe King was the iceman. He showed up regularly all year long to bring ice for the icebox. Even though Abby's family drove a car, an old Nash with curtains in the backseat windows, Joe still arrived in a horse-drawn cart. He would hop out, use a pick to chip a block of ice off an even bigger block of ice, and haul it into the Nicholses' house over his shoulder, his clothing protected by a rubber cape. Then he deposited the ice in a pan in the icebox. Sometimes in hot weather he would give Abby and Rose each a sliver of ice, which they held in their bare hands and licked like lollipops while the water ran down their wrists.

Abby finished her oatmeal and cleared the kitchen table. Outside, the wind roared and the snow fell, and from the other side of the house came the sound of Pop's hammer. Mama placed a bowl of potatoes in front of Abby and she tackled them with a sigh. Peeling potatoes was her least favorite chore, but Mama didn't think Rose was old enough to handle a knife, so the chore fell to Abby.

"We'll turn on the Victrola," said Mama. "We can listen to music while we work."

Rachmaninoff was playing in the background and Abby was peeling and Rose's hands were sticky with biscuit dough and Mama was adding more kindling to the woodstove when the lights first flickered.

"Uh-oh," said Abby. She glanced outside for the millionth time and watched the snowflakes swirl through the gloom.

"I think I'd better ring up Betty," said Mama, and just as the words left her mouth, the phone jangled on the little table outside the kitchen. Rose leaped to answer it, but Mama got there first, and Abby listened to her mother's end of the conversation. "Yes, yes, I thought as much. . . . No, of course not. . . . I know. The girls will be very disappointed. . . . All that food. . . . Well, there's nothing to be done. . . . All right. . . . All right. . . . Happy Thanksgiving to you."

Mama hung up the phone and Rose burst into tears.

"I'm sorry, Rose," said Mama, and she put her arms around Rose's thin shoulders.

The hammering had stopped and Pop appeared in the kitchen doorway. "Was that Betty?" he asked, and the lights flickered again. They flickered on and off two more times and finally went out.

"The electrical lines must have gone down," said Pop. "I'm not surprised."

"This is exciting!" Abby declared. "It's like the olden days! No electric lights."

"And all this food," said Mama. "Enough for ten people. Well, there's nothing to do but finish cooking it."

"Please, may I call Sarah?" asked Abby, who normally wasn't allowed to do so, since Sarah lived just three doors away and Abby could run there easily.

"I suppose," replied Pop, and that was when Abby discovered that the phone lines were down, too.

"Ooh, scary!" she said.

"Ooh, scary!" echoed Rose, sounding more cheerful.

Pop lit two kerosene lamps and Abby returned to the potatoes. "I've done half, Mama," she said.

"Better stop there. Put the others back in the bin. We won't need nearly so many now."

Abby gratefully returned the unpeeled potatoes to the wooden bin and turned to the blueberry pies.

"Are those blueberries the ones we picked with Orrin last —" Rose started to say, and then looked guiltily over her shoulder.

"Hush," Abby whispered urgently, but it was too late.

Pop had turned away from the kitchen, but now he turned back and stood once again in the doorway. "What did you say, Rose?"

"Nothing."

"Rose?"

"I was just wondering if . . ." Rose glanced helplessly at Abby, who looked at Mama, who bowed her head.

"Yes?" said Pop.

"Well, I was wondering if those were the blueberries we picked last summer."

"I thought I heard Orrin's name mentioned."

Rose stared out the window.

"Because you know you aren't allowed to" — Pop paused — "to consort with him."

"Yes, sir," said Rose. "I mean, no, sir."

Pop hesitated, then walked away, and soon Abby could hear hammering again. Into the silence of the kitchen, she said, "Mama, should I make the fancy crust for the pies?" Without waiting for an answer she began slicing the dough into strips and patting it down on the filling in a crisscross pattern. "Just like at the bakery!" she announced.

Rose let out her breath and Mama began to move dishes in and out of the icebox and in and out of the gas oven. The house smelled first like turkey, and then like turkey and cranberries, and then like turkey and cranberries and stuffing, and then like all those things plus cooling pies.

Rose had just complained that she was bored when Abby heard a sound that was a little like thunder and a little like a crack of lightning, and she looked out the window in time to see a tree that had bent in the force of the wind suddenly snap in two, the top part falling behind the Becketts' house next door. It landed gently, sending up great puffs of snow in a line stretching from the edge of the woods to the Becketts' back stoop.

Rose screamed and ran to Mama, but Abby stared at the broken trunk and the whirling flakes and felt her heart quicken. She watched as Mr. Beckett appeared on his stoop, looked at the tree, then up to the sky, shook his head, and closed his door again. The tree would remain where it lay, covered sometimes with snow, sometimes with sleet, sometimes just with frost, until April when Mr. Beckett would finally saw through the damp trunk.

"What a Thanksgiving," said Mama, holding Rose tight.

"It's a horrible Thanksgiving," replied Rose.

"Then let's make it better." Abby opened the kitchen cupboard and brought out the tin box of crayons and the scraps of butcher paper. "We should make place mats, Rose. And place cards, like for a fancy dinner in a rich person's house."

Rose pulled away from Mama. "Okay."

Abby and her sister sat and colored by the light of a kerosene lamp, and sometimes Abby watched Rose's face, and she thought about the late afternoon when Rose had been born and Mama, exhausted, had looked across the bedroom at the jar of flowers on the windowsill and seen the single rose that Pop had added to the bouquet and said to herself, "I'm going to name this baby Rose."

And so Rose's entire name was Rose Nichols. But Abby had been named for her two grandmothers — Abigail and Cora — and so her entire name was Abigail Cora Nichols.

Abby printed her name carefully now, her full name, at the bottom of the place mat she had made for Pop — a drawing of a beautiful living turkey in between an Indian and a Pilgrim.

Later, when the place mats and place cards were finished and the kitchen table had been set and the dishes piled with turkey and stuffing and potatoes, Pop glared at Abby, whose fork was already halfway to her mouth, and said, "Let's remember who provided us with this meal." Then he bowed his head and Abby set down her fork and everyone joined hands. "Heavenly Father," Pop began, "we thank You for Your bountiful blessings. . . ."

Once when it had been Rose's turn to say the blessing, she had chanted, "Yum, yum, thanks for the food, God. Amen." And Pop had whacked her bottom with a book.

"Let's tell Thanksgiving stories," said Abby after Pop had said "amen."

"What kind of Thanksgiving stories?" asked Rose.

"Things that happened a long time ago."

Pop told about the first time he had killed a turkey all by himself and how proud he'd been, but how his little brother had cried and cried at the sight of the dead bird and said he wouldn't eat the turkey. And he hadn't. (Abby thought this was a horrible story.)

Mama told about her first Thanksgiving with Pop, before he had finished building their house, when they were living with Mama's parents. "I stood up at the end of the meal and said, 'Thanksgiving is certainly going to be different next year.' And your pop said, 'That's right. We'll be in our new house.' And I said, 'And there will be three people living in it.'"

"And that's how Pop found out that I was going to be born, right?" said Abby.

"That's right."

Then Abby told the story of the very first Thanksgiving ever, which she had learned in school, and finally Rose told a story about how she had once ridden a horse through a blizzard on Thanksgiving Day in order to deliver a turkey to a poor family whose tree had fallen down, and Pop said something about falsehoods, but he didn't look too mad.

"I think this was the best Thanksgiving ever," Abby whispered to her sister that night, as they lay in their bed again.

Beyond the window the moon shone and the stars shone and the last of the clouds were scudding across the sky, blown by a brisk, biting wind. Downstairs, the snow was piled right up to the windowsills, and Pop was going to have to shovel his way out the front door in the morning. But for now all the Nicholses were safe and warm in their beds.

"The *best* Thanksgiving?" Rose repeated.

"Well, the most exciting."

Abby knew she would remember this day always. And when she was grown, when she was a very old woman, she would tell the story of the Thanksgiving storm to her grandchildren and they would ask question after question about woodstoves and iceboxes and kerosene lamps and the Great Depression and wonder how Abby had ever survived the olden days.

Chapter 3

Abby sat between Rose and Sarah in the backseat of Pop's Nash, giggling every time the car rode over a bump and they were jounced toward the roof. She leaned into the front seat. "Pop, can we get ice cream when we're in Barnegat Point?" she asked.

"I'm not made of money," Pop replied, which didn't mean either yes or no.

A trip to Barnegat Point was always exciting. It was a real town with a main street and shops and a movie theatre and a bakery and a doctor's office and a drugstore with a soda fountain — unlike Lewisport, with its general store and, well, that was pretty much it. Abby went to school in Barnegat Point. All the Lewisport children did, since there was no school in their village. But the Barnegat Point school was two blocks from the main street and Pop always dropped Abby and Rose off in a big hurry on his way to his carpentry shop. They rarely had a chance to walk around the town.

Now Rose leaned forward. "But can we get ice cream?" she wanted to know.

"We'll see," said Pop. "First I have to go to the house and check on the supplies that were delivered."

Pop had a job doing carpentry work on a big house that some people from New York City were building. It was going to be their summer home, and Pop had been hired to make all the cabinets and cupboards and bookshelves.

"Wait till you see this place," said Pop proudly. "It will be finished before winter, and it's going to be grand. It has six bedrooms and four bathrooms —"

It was Sarah's turn to lean forward. "Four bathrooms? How many people are going to live in the house?"

"Five, I think," Pop replied.

Abby and Sarah looked at each other. "Almost everyone has their own bathroom," commented Abby.

"Yuh," said Pop. "They're building the house right on the ocean, too."

"Our house is near the ocean," said Rose.

"This is different," said Pop. "These people own the beach in front of their house, and they have a view of the harbor and all up and down the coast. And everything I'm building is very fancy — ornate — because that's the way they like things. Nothing but the best. They're going to have maids."

"Like Hannah Gruen? Nancy Drew's housekeeper?" asked Abby, who had borrowed *The Secret of the Old Clock* from the library over the summer.

Pop shrugged. "I guess. Now listen. When we get to the house I have to check on the materials, and I don't want you girls to touch anything. You can look but don't touch. And don't go upstairs or anywhere I can't see you, okay? This is a very fancy place."

Pop urged the Nash along the coast road until a large, half-finished structure came into view.

"That's as big as — as a castle!" exclaimed Abby.

"Well, it's a mansion anyway," said Pop with pride.

He turned off the road and parked the car in the drive behind the house.

"How come the house is backward?" asked Sarah. "It's facing the wrong way. It's got its back to the road."

"Its front is facing the ocean," Pop replied, happy to be able to answer the question. "That's the way rich people like things. Facing the view."

"We face the ocean," said Rose in a small voice.

"Not the same thing," Pop said flatly. "There's a road between our house and that stretch of beach we don't own."

Sarah climbed out of the car, followed by Abby and Rose.

Pop stood and looked at the house, shaking his head with

pride. "They asked me to build them some furniture, too," he said.

Abby was gaping at the grand structure, with its wings and porches and doors opening onto patios. "What . . . Who *are* these people?" she finally asked.

"Nice rich family," Pop replied. "Churchgoing Protestants. Republicans. Industrious. Born and raised here in the US. Family's been here for generations. They know how to make money and they know how to spend it. They have taste."

Abby thought of the tiny house on Blue Harbor Lane and of her parents, who dispensed nickels so carefully. She thought of Mama making dresses for her and Rose because handmade was cheaper than store bought, and she thought of Pop and his carpentry jobs. Pop worked and worked and was also very industrious, but still money was scarce. What did that say about Pop and Mama? Abby wondered. But she knew better than to ask.

Pop walked around to the side of the house, where a pile of lumber had been delivered. He bent and examined it, while Abby peered through an open doorway into the house. "Sarah!" she called. "Rose! Come here. You have to see this staircase. It curls around like a snail shell."

Rose and Sarah piled behind Abby and gawked at the steps.

"Did you build the staircase, Pop?" asked Abby.

"Made the balusters. Every one of them. And they're my own design. When the lady in the family saw them, that was when she asked me to build some furniture — two dressers and four spindle-back chairs."

Abby and Rose and Sarah walked along the front of the house, staying in Pop's line of sight. Abby turned to her right. "You can see the lighthouse from here!"

"I bet you can see all the way up to Bar Harbor," said Sarah, shading her eyes and peering in the other direction.

"Really?" said Abby, squinting into the sun.

"Well, maybe not. But far."

"Girls!" Pop called then. "Time to go."

Pop drove the Nash into town. He hummed as he drove, and he tapped his hands on the steering wheel. The house had put him in a good mood and Abby hoped he would stay that way.

Pop was a mystery to Abby. She had never met his parents, although she knew they lived in Connecticut. She wasn't sure what had brought her pop to Maine, just that he had arrived in 1918, not long before he had met Mama. Abby didn't like to ask him too many questions, because too many questions annoyed him. So she sometimes asked Mama questions about Pop, on the days when Mama didn't seem too sad about the rosebushes and the babies who hadn't lived.

Abby squirmed in the backseat and traded places with Sarah in order to sit by the window.

"Close your eyes!" shrieked Rose, who was sitting by the other window. "We're going by the school. Nobody look at it!" Second grade had not gotten off to a good start for Rose.

Abby dutifully closed her eyes, but opened them again so she wouldn't miss the first sight of Barnegat Point's main street. A minute later Pop turned left and there it was. The squat buildings — made of wood except for the bank, which was brick — sat close to the street, and Abby read the signs as they passed them: Drugs, Launderette, Peake's Jewelry, Treat's Market, Optometrist, F. D. Haworth's (that was a clothing store), Strand Theater.

"Pop?" said Rose.

And Pop replied, "Don't ask me again about ice cream or the answer will be no."

No one said a word while Pop parked the car. Then they piled out, and Abby looked up and down the street. American flags hung above most of the shops. Mr. Peake stood smoking a cigar in front of his jewelry store. A skinny cat peered out from under a truck, then darted into an alley, tail twitching.

"I love Barnegat Point," Sarah ventured, glancing at Pop, who said nothing.

"Oh!" exclaimed Abby. "Sarah, there's Marie!" Abby waved at a dark-haired girl sitting on a bench in front of the launderette. "Marie! Marie!"

Marie grinned and waved back. The girls were in fourth grade together and Marie knew all the best rhymes for skipping rope, and had also taught Abby and Sarah how to French braid their hair.

"Hi," said Abby, running to her. "What are you doing here?"

Marie angled her head toward the launderette. "Waiting for my mother."

"Do you —" Abby started to say, but a hand grabbed her elbow then and jerked her down the street. She looked up at Pop as he hurried her away. "What's wrong?" she asked. Pop's face frightened her.

"I told you I don't want you associating with those French kids." He paused. "Or with Catholics."

Abby came to a halt and jerked away from Pop, but all she said was "Marie isn't French."

Pop glared at her. "Don't sass me. Her parents came from Quebec. They're immigrants. They don't talk English at home. And they're Catholics. There's no need for you to associate with them."

"But I go to school with Marie! She's in my class." Abby could hear her voice trembling. She marched ahead of Pop, who caught up with her quickly.

"That's bad enough. You don't have to talk to her outside of school." Pop glanced over his shoulder at Rose and Sarah, who were following cautiously. He lowered his voice. "And you don't need to be spending so much time with Orrin either. I keep telling you that."

Abby felt anger surge from some unidentifiable part of her body, threatening to explode. She took a breath. "But he lives right down the street," she said at last. "We've known each other since we were five."

"Still doesn't mean you have to spend any time with him."

"What's *wrong* with him?"

"I've told you. His mother's a foreigner. And a Catholic. And Orrin is born of her, so that makes him an Irish Catholic, too."

Abby stomped her foot. "But Orrin's nice —"

"I don't care. Him and his people are spoiling the population. Maine should be white —"

"Orrin's white," said Abby quietly. "So is Marie." She shook her head and looked away from Pop. She felt suddenly the way she had felt when she'd seen Pop kick Sarah's cat one day when he thought no one was looking.

"Maybe so, but let me finish. They're not American. And they're not Protestant. Our people here should be all those things. You are, and be thankful for it. Another thing about Orrin — his father can't keep a job. His mother doesn't work either. No excuse for that. They're able-bodied. Nothing wrong with either of them."

"But his mother's Irish Catholic. I thought you said that means there *is* something wrong with her."

Pop looked sharply at Abby. "I hope you aren't making fun," he said.

"No."

"Because Orrin's mother could wash clothes or dishes. Something. There are plenty of jobs for the lower classes. She's just lazy. So's Orrin's father. Now take me. I don't come from much, but I work hard and my business is taking off. I'm making something of myself. I'm going to have a big business one day. Soon, too. There are better families than Orrin's, Abigail, and better families than that girl's."

"Her name is Marie."

"One more word," said Pop. "Just one more word."

Abby closed her mouth. She slowed her pace until she was walking with Sarah and Rose, and Pop was walking ahead by himself. Sarah put her arm around Abby.

Abby breathed in the salty air and the fishy smell from Treat's, and the sugary smell from the bakery, and the warm sun smell. She looked up at the clear blue sky and ahead to where the road rose slightly and then seemed to fall away into the ocean.

"*Animal Crackers* is playing at the movies," said Rose, but she said it in a whisper in case the notion should annoy Pop for some reason. "Maybe we'll get to go."

Abby glanced at Pop, who was entering the hardware store. "Maybe in a couple of years, when Pop's as rich as he says he's going to be."

"What?" said Rose.

Abby shook her head. "Nothing." She couldn't explain Pop. Not to Rose and not even to herself. She wanted to punish him, but couldn't think of anything that wouldn't lead to Pop punishing her back.

Pop came out of the hardware store carrying a paper bag full of nails and smiling, because the store was run by Mike Connell, who was white and a Republican and went to the Methodist church. "Who wants ice cream?" he asked.

Abby wanted to jump up and down and cry, "Me!" but she was smarting from her conversation with Pop. So instead she walked sedately along the street with Sarah until they reached the drugstore, where Pop ordered four vanilla ice-cream cones. Then they walked through Barnegat Point, Abby and Sarah licking at their cones delicately, Pop eating his in great chunks, and Rose biting off the tip of her cone and slurping the ice cream down through the hole. Pop pointed out three of the larger houses in town and then began talking about the summer people again, and Abby stopped listening. She daydreamed about living by herself in the lighthouse and inviting Orrin and Marie to visit her whenever she felt like company.

The afternoon, which had felt ruined, got better the moment Abby and Rose and Pop walked through the door of their cottage in Lewisport.

Mama greeted them with a smile, drying her hands on a dishrag. "Betty called while you were in town," she said. "They're coming over for supper. They'll be here soon."

"All of them?" asked Abby, and her heart leaped.

Behind her she heard Rose gulp in air, a sure sign she was about to start practicing her burping.

"All of them," said Mama.

Long before the sun started to sink out of view, Abby and Rose, Blaine, Erma, Karl, and Dorothy (the cousins who were older than twelve), and Sarah, Emily, Douglas, and half the kids from Blue Harbor Lane, but not Orrin, who knew better, were playing baseball in Abby's yard. Blaine had made himself the umpire and the coach and was teaching the younger kids how to pitch and hit and also how to burp and spit. Abby felt the last of the sun on her face, and the sticky, salty air, and had just hit Blaine's baseball with a satisfying crack when Mama leaned out the door and called, "Girls, come help with supper, please," so Abby, Rose, Erma, and Dorothy had to excuse themselves from the game.

There was plenty to do in the kitchen, and Abby liked helping Mama and Aunt Betty, while Pop and Uncle Marshall sat in the front room by an open window with their cigarettes, letting the smoke drift out into the yard.

Supper that night was a beach picnic, everyone helping to carry chicken and corn and pies and lemonade across the road and across the sand, settling on the beach that didn't belong to them. Sarah's cat, Patches, joined them for part of the supper, begging scraps of food until Pop swatted her rump and Patches hissed at him and ran back across the road.

After supper, Pop disappeared into the storage shed and returned with the horseshoes and stakes. The boys played horseshoes on the beach while the girls and Mama and Aunt Betty cleaned up the kitchen.

"I'll teach you to play cribbage," Erma said to Abby and Rose later. "I brought our board."

Abby, Rose, Erma, and Dorothy sat on the little front porch and studied their game by the light of a kerosene lamp. From the beach came shouts from the horseshoe players and the occasional cry of a gull. Mama moved quietly through the house, bringing tea to Aunt Betty, taking out the hidden tin of caramels, checking on the girls, and once, only once, looking out the back window in the direction of the rosebushes.

When Rose's head began to nod sleepily over the cribbage board, Mama picked her up from her chair and said it looked like the day was done. Aunt Betty called across the street to the horseshoe players, and soon Uncle Marshall's car was driving slowly down Blue Harbor Lane, Blaine leaning out the back window and calling, "Abby, you're the best girl pitcher I know," which made her beam with pride.

Long after Mama and Pop had gone to bed downstairs, Abby lay awake next to Rose, breathing in her sister's smell of caramel and Ipana toothpaste and seawater and also rosewater, since Rose had stolen some of Mama's so that she would smell nice for Blaine.

Across the street, on the other side of the sea grass, the waves rolled onto the sand. Abby could tell, just by the way the air felt in the room, that a fog would come in off the ocean during the night and that by the next morning she wouldn't be able to see the Becketts' house next door.

She turned over carefully and thought about Marie and about Orrin and the Umhays, and about what it must feel like to be foreign or dark-skinned or out of work when all around you, people like Pop were watching with smug eyes.

Chapter 4

"Abby . . . Abby? . . . *Abby!*"

"What? Rose, I'm sleeping."

"But it's morning. And there are only six days until Christmas. That's less than a week."

"I know."

"Well, do you think Santa Claus will come?"

"Today?"

"No, on Christmas Eve."

"Yes."

"What if he doesn't?"

"He always does."

"Do you think he got our letters?"

"I don't know. Yes."

"Really?"

"Yes."

Rose sat up in bed. "Oh, I hope he got mine. I only asked

for one thing, like Pop said. So I wasn't being greedy." She leaned forward and sniffed. "Mama's baking!"

Abby sat up quickly. "I smell gingerbread."

"Hey, it's snowing!" cried Rose.

"This is perfect. Christmas and snow and gingerbread."

"And presents," added Rose.

Signs of Christmas were everywhere. In the homes on Blue Harbor Lane, decorated trees stood by windows, and in Hammer's, the general store, Abby and Rose had looked longingly at a box labeled THE TWELVE DAYS OF CHRISTMAS, which held twelve intricate glass tree ornaments.

"Don't touch!" Mr. Hammer barked every time he caught sight of Abby and Rose, even though they were careful to do nothing but look around the crowded store. Abby even clasped her mittened hands behind her back. At this time of year some of the shelves that usually held tools and fishing line and oilskin coats had been stocked with far more tempting items: peppermint sticks and ginger cookies and toys. There were teddy bears and Raggedy Ann dolls, as well as a play wristwatch (which was what Rose had asked Santa for) and a toy horse with a saddle (which was what Abby had asked Santa for).

And there was a tea set, a tiny tea set almost like the one Rose had tried to win at the ring toss the year before. Abby didn't think her sister had seen it, since Mr. Hammer displayed it on a shelf with stacks of sturdy, practical cups and saucers (in regular size), not with the toys. And this was perfect, because Abby planned to surprise her sister with the tea set on Christmas morning. She imagined Rose bouncing down the stairs before the sun had risen, unable to wait any longer, and running first to her stocking to make sure there wasn't any coal in it, and then to the tree to look for her present from Santa. Under the tree she would see the little box with the tag on it reading TO ROSE, LOVE ABBY and she would tear the paper off and find a perfect china tea set.

The tea set cost eighty-nine cents and Abby had been saving her money since the moment she'd spotted the teensy cups and saucers and teapot on Mr. Hammer's back shelf. She'd had forty cents in her bank then, and ever since she'd been offering to mend clothes for Mama and to do chores for Pop. When she had seventy-nine cents saved up, she sold her shell barrette to Sarah for the final ten cents, making Sarah promise never to wear it in front of Mama or Pop. That had been yesterday, and now the eighty-nine cents (one dime, eight nickels, and thirty-nine pennies) were in her bank, which she had shoved into the back of her dresser drawer.

Abby turned away from the window, dressed quickly in her warmest clothes, and ran downstairs to the kitchen, Rose at her heels.

Mama was stirring gingerbread in a milky white bowl, and the kitchen smelled of molasses and cinnamon and ginger and cloves.

"Can I lick the bowl?" asked Abby.

"After breakfast," Mama replied.

Pop leaned in through the doorway. "I'm going to the workshop for a while," he said. "When I get back, we can go look for a tree."

"Really?" said Abby. "Today?" Christmas and snow and gingerbread and a tree.

And her secret plan.

"As soon as I get back," said Pop. And off he went, clapping his hat on his head.

"Pop sure is working a lot lately," commented Abby from her place at the table.

"Business is doing well," Mama replied, and she sounded proud. "We're lucky. Lots of people are out of work, but your father is doing better than ever."

After Pop had made the furniture for the summer people from New York City, other people had begun giving him orders for furniture. He had a workshop in Barnegat Point where he now employed four very grateful men. Furthermore, in addition to the Nash, he owned a truck, and across each side of the truck he had painted the words *Luther Nichols, Furniture Maker* in very fancy letters.

"Imagine," Abby had heard her mother say to Sarah's mother a few months earlier. "His own workshop with *four* employees. And he's not just a carpenter, he's a *furniture maker.*"

Sarah's mother had replied, "He's an artist."

Abby wasn't sure about that, but she did know that Pop was a little freer with nickels and dimes these days. He had given Mama money to buy new shoes for Abby and Rose before their old ones had worn out, plus enough money for new winter coats. Then he had bought Mama a brand-new stove and a little iron bench for the yard. Before the weather had turned cold, Mama would sometimes sit out on the bench and look at the rosebushes.

Pop had a bank account in Barnegat Point now, too. "Getting fat," he had remarked one evening to Mama, and Abby, horrified, had thought Pop was insulting Mama, before she'd realized he meant that the bank account was getting fat, not her.

"Mama?" Rose said now, standing up from the table to look longingly into the mixing bowl and sniff the gingerbread batter. "Why don't grown-ups ask Santa for presents?"

Mama smiled. "Because Santa is a toy maker and grown-ups just want boring things like stoves and sweaters."

"What do *you* want for Christmas?" asked Abby.

"Oh, goodness. Nothing. I have you and Rose and your father. That's enough for me."

"No, it isn't. You want another baby," said Rose, and Abby kicked her sister under the table. They were not supposed to mention babies around Mama.

Mama turned away and looked out the window. After a moment she said, "A new scarf would be nice."

Abby brightened. That was perfect. She had secretly been knitting a scarf for her mother and it was nearly finished.

She pushed her chair back and stood up.

"Where are you going?" asked Rose as Abby began climbing the stairs to their bedroom. "Don't you want to lick the bowl?"

"You can have it all."

"Really?"

"Really." Upstairs, Abby sat on the bed and dumped out the money from her bank. She counted it again. She had eighty-nine cents exactly. She found her plaid change purse, the one on the chain, and she poured her pennies and nickels and the dime into it. It weighed more than she had expected and was fatter than she had expected, too.

Abby looked out the window at the snow. The smell of gingerbread drifted up from the kitchen and she felt her stomach flip-flop with excitement. It was Christmastime and she was about to leave on her secret errand.

Getting out of the house was easier than she had thought it would be. She pulled on her outdoor clothes as fast as possible, called, "Going to Sarah's," over her shoulder, and ran out the door.

The route to Hammer's took her through the pine woods, where she breathed in the scent of a thousand Christmas trees and stopped to watch snow fall on the deep green branches. A chickadee swooped ahead of her along the path. Abby scuffed through the snow and stuck out her tongue to catch snowflakes.

Eighty-nine cents, she thought. She hoped Mr. Hammer hadn't raised the price of the tea set. Then she had another thought that made her stop in the middle of the woods and say, "Oh no!" aloud. She hadn't been to Hammer's in over a week. What if the tea set had been sold? What if someone was buying it at that very moment?

Abby quickened her pace. She emerged from the woods on the other side of the little spit of land, turned left, reached Lewisport Road, and hurried by Mr. Harrison's fishing shack, and the falling-down house where Toby Hopper lived with his big brother and no parents, and then the house that belonged to Mr. Hammer and his wife. Finally, just beyond their house, was Hammer's itself.

On this dark, snowy day the lighted window glowed warmly. Abby paused in front of it and pretended to inspect the electric train that ran around and around a jumbled display of cookware. She wanted to purchase the tea set as fast as possible, but she had to consider how to approach Mr. Hammer. She hated talking to him. He called her "little girl," although he knew her name, and he never quite seemed to trust her. Abby was certain he was not going to be happy about counting out thirty-nine pennies, even if no one else was in the store.

At last Abby opened the door and stepped inside, brushing snow off of her coat sleeves and shaking more snow off of her hat. She stuffed her hat and mittens in her pocket and looked at the counter where Mr. Hammer was standing behind the wooden cash register, ringing up a sale of flour and sugar to Toby Hopper. The cash register dinged, the drawer opened, and Mr. Hammer deposited Toby's dollar bill in the drawer and handed him his change. Toby dropped the change down into his boot, glanced awkwardly at Abby, and fled from the store.

"What can I help you with, little girl?" called Mr. Hammer as Abby made her way to the back of the store. "Don't touch anything!"

"I won't." Abby squeezed her eyes shut as she approached the shelf with the display of cups and saucers. Then she opened them slowly. There were the adult-size cups, the adult-size saucers . . . and the tea set in a box.

Abby reached for it.

"No touching!" shouted Mr. Hammer, who had crept up behind her.

Abby jumped. "But," she said, "but . . . I want to buy that. The tea set. It's a present for Rose. My sister. And I have enough money. It's all here." She unbuttoned her coat and held out the fat change purse.

Mr. Hammer paused. "It costs eighty-nine cents."

"I know. I've been saving."

"I'd better go count it." Mr. Hammer slid the tea set off the shelf, turned, and threaded his way to the front of the shop. Abby followed him, stopping only once to look at the horse and saddle.

When Mr. Hammer reached the counter, he placed the tea set on it and held out his hand. Abby emptied her coins into it. They spilled over the outstretched hand and onto the counter. Mr. Hammer muttered, "Jeez Louise," and started counting.

"Eighty-seven, eighty-eight, eighty-nine," he said a minute later.

Abby almost replied, "I told you so," but she didn't want to do anything to jinx Rose's present.

Mr. Hammer didn't say another word, but he did wrap each tiny cup and saucer, the teapot, and its lid in tissue paper. Then he placed all the little bundles back in the box and handed it to Abby.

"Thank you," she whispered, and fled from the store.

She met Sarah halfway through the woods, the snow falling thickly now, the late morning nearly as dark as evening.

Abby thrust the box at her friend. "I got it! It was still there and I had exactly enough money. Thanks to your dime!"

Sarah opened her mouth, and then closed it again, and in that instant, Abby's excitement rushed out of her like air from a pricked balloon. One of the advantages of having a best friend was being able to hold conversations without words, and Abby and Sarah had been best friends for a long time. So Abby knew something was wrong even before Sarah said, "That's great, but, Abby, your father is looking for you. He's mad."

Abby took the box back and put it in her pocket. "Why is he mad?"

"You said you were going to my house, so he went looking for you there, and I didn't know where you were."

"Uh-oh. How mad is he?"

Sarah winced. She knew Pop's temper almost as well as Abby and Rose did. "Mad. Just go home."

Abby ran back through the woods ahead of Sarah. She met her father walking briskly along Blue Harbor Lane. He did not look happy.

"Where were you?" he demanded.

"I —" Abby began. She wanted badly to keep Rose's gift a surprise until Christmas Day. "It's a secret. But I didn't do anything bad. Honest."

"You disobeyed me."

Abby didn't remember Pop forbidding her to leave the house, but she said, "I'm sorry," anyway.

"And you lied," Pop went on. "You told your mother you were going to Sarah's."

"I'm sorry," Abby said again. "I thought I would be back in time. And this is a really important secret. Not a bad thing. You'll find out what it is. On Christmas Day."

Pop looked at her with hard eyes. "No. Lying. Do you understand me?"

"Yes, sir."

Abby's punishment was that she wasn't allowed to go with Pop, Mama, and Rose to choose the tree. But she found that she didn't mind as much as she had thought she would. She sat by herself in the kitchen with Christmas carols playing on the Victrola, and she wrapped the tea set in red paper and tied the box with a white hair ribbon. Pop couldn't stop her from doing that. He couldn't control everything.

When Rose opened the box on Christmas morning, she burst into tears and asked Abby over and over how she had managed to get the tea set from the mean traveling-fair man. And when Rose was a grown-up — this was two decades later — she passed the tea set down to her own daughters one snowy Christmas morning and told them about the traveling fair and Mr. Hammer and Aunt Abby's secret plan.

Chapter 5

Abby woke with a start, and before she had opened her eyes, she thought, *This is the last time I'll wake up in this room.* She decided to say her thought out loud: "This is the last time I'll wake up in this room."

"No, it isn't," said Rose from beside her.

Abby rolled over and looked at her sister. "I didn't know you were up."

"I can't sleep."

"Are you sad?"

"No, I'm happy! We don't have to go to school today. Anyway, this is *not* the last time we'll wake up in this room. You know this is going to be our beach cottage from now on. Pop said we can spend lots of time here in the summer."

Pop, Abby thought, was the only Nichols who truly wanted to move to Barnegat Point, into the second-largest house on their new street. He was proud of this accomplishment, but Abby didn't want to leave Blue Harbor Lane, and neither did

Mama. Rose was excited about the new house, but really, Rose was happy wherever she was.

"I know," said Abby. "But it won't be the same. Our real house will be in Barnegat Point. We'll wake up there most mornings — and what will I see when I look out my window?"

Rose shrugged. A view was a view. She wasn't sure why Abby cared so much about it. "I don't know. What?"

"Well, I don't know either. But it won't be the ocean. It will probably just be the house next door."

Rose shrugged again.

"Won't you miss the ocean?" Abby asked. She couldn't imagine living without the sound of the waves, a sound as natural to her as a heartbeat.

"I guess. But, Abby, we get to live in town. In a big house! We'll each have our own room. Even the baby will have its own room, after it's born. And there are *two* bathrooms. And a dining room. And a parlor." Rose paused. "What's a parlor anyway?"

It's a room for people who want to show off that they're rich, Abby thought. But what she said was, "It's like a living room, but I think it's fancier and you're supposed to entertain guests in it."

"Well, whatever it is, I don't care. We don't have to go to school today!"

Abby sighed. She knew that eventually she'd get used to the idea of the fancy house in Barnegat Point, but she would miss the cottage by the sea.

"Girls!" called Mama from downstairs. "Hurry up now. Today is a big day!"

The move to Barnegat Point was going to be easy. Abby remembered when the Becketts had moved into the cottage next door. Every stick of their furniture and all their belongings had been packed in a truck and it had taken hours to unload everything. But the Nicholses were leaving most of their belongings in the cottage that would become their beach house, and Mama and Pop had bought all new things for the house in town. Abby and Rose would need to unpack their clothes and organize their rooms, but that was about it.

Abby, wearing a pale blue dress (a present for her tenth birthday) and matching blue socks, clattered downstairs in her lace-up shoes and found Mama standing at the back window, hands resting on her spreading belly, watching Pop as he supervised the digging up of the rosebushes, which would be making the trip to the new yard in Barnegat Point.

"Eat something quickly," said Mama, turning from the window. "Your father wants us in the car in half an hour."

Abby wondered whether Pop was more excited about the new house or the new baby. It was a thought she kept to herself.

Fifteen minutes later, Abby said a secret good-bye to Orrin. She found him on the beach in front of his house, standing ankle deep in frigid seawater, staring at the horizon.

"I'll see you every day in school, you know," she told him.

Orrin nodded. "But still. Everything is going to change. Now we'll only get to see each other in school. What are we going to do all summer?"

Abby sighed. "We'll figure something out. We'll still come back here. We're keeping our old house."

Orrin shrugged. "It won't be the same."

"I know."

When Orrin said nothing more, Abby leaned forward, kissed him on the cheek as quick as the flash of a lightning bug, and fled from the beach. She was not about to let Orrin Umhay see her cry.

Her secret good-bye with Orrin was followed by a regular good-bye with Sarah, and she started off by telling her what she'd told Orrin earlier: "We'll still get to see each other in school."

Sarah was already blinking back tears. "I'm going to miss you anyway. You've lived three doors away from me for as long as I can remember."

"Well," said Abby, drawing a handkerchief from her pocket and swiping at her eyes, "now you can come to Barnegat Point to visit me. And some days maybe you can come home with me after school. We can be town girls. We can go to the movies and get ice cream and look in the stores."

"But it won't be as good as having you here all the time."

Abby reached for Sarah, gave her a fast, fierce hug, and ran down Blue Harbor Lane.

"See you in school tomorrow!" Sarah called after her.

Abby waved over her shoulder. And in no time, it seemed, Pop was swinging the Nicholses' new Buick Roadster onto Haddon Road in Barnegat Point. Abby, even though she had been on Haddon many times, scrambled over Rose for a better look at the house that was now their home.

"It's so big," said Rose softly.

"I know," Abby replied. And their new house (which was actually almost fifteen years old) *was* big. But it was not the biggest house on the street. And it certainly wasn't as big as the summer houses on the beach, the houses for the people from New York and Boston. But still.

Pop passed the house that *was* the largest on the street, the one with two turrets and three floors, and turned into the drive next door.

You could fit our old house and Sarah's house right down inside our new one, Abby thought, *and still have plenty of space left over.*

Pop parked the Buick at the top of the drive, and Abby and Rose jumped out of the car and ran through the front door of the house. They were greeted by Ellen, a cheerful, rosy-cheeked woman, older than Mama, who was wearing a white apron over a gray dress. Ellen was their new housekeeper, something Mama said she would never, ever get used to.

"You mean we won't have to make our beds?" Abby had asked when Pop had announced that he'd hired Ellen — along with Mike, who was to help with the yard and the Buick, and Sheila, who was to help Ellen until the baby came. Then she would be the baby's nurse.

"I mean no such thing at all," said Mama. "You girls still have your chores."

Pop had frowned at Mama. "For heaven's sake, Nell," he'd said. "I can afford help now. You don't think Stuart Burley makes his kids do chores, do you?" Stuart Burley owned the two-turreted house next door. "Burley's got help, just like us. That's what people do when they have this much money. They hire help so their wives don't have to cook and clean, and their kids can hold their heads up when they walk into town."

Mama had said nothing to this. But now she called Abby and Rose back outside. "Before you do anything else, girls, you need to unpack your clothes."

Pop threw Mama an angry look and turned back to Abby and Rose. "And then you have the rest of the day off."

"Gosh, we could have gone to school," Abby said.

Rose pinched her arm and Abby squeaked, but said nothing further.

"Mike will bring your suitcases inside," Pop added pointedly.

While she waited for the suitcases, Abby walked cautiously through the rooms on the ground floor of the house. The front door opened into a hall, and through the first door on the left was what Pop said was the parlor, the entertaining room. It was furnished with pieces from Barnegat Interior, and with chairs and tables from Pop's own company. Across the hall from the parlor was a similar room, just not quite as fancy, and in the back of the house were the kitchen, the dining room, and Pop's study.

"What do you think he's going to study?" Rose asked Abby as they peeped through the door.

"Nothing. It's like an office."

"It doesn't look like an office. It looks like a library. Except with no books on the shelves. I've never seen a desk like that in an office." Rose eyed the rolltop desk that had also come from Pop's company.

"Well, it's still an office."

Abby left Rose, walked back to the hall, and began to climb the stairs to the second floor. The staircase didn't curve like a snail shell, the way the one in the summer house did, but there was a landing partway up where Pop said they should put a table with a statue on it. At the top of the stairs was another hall, and from this opened the doors to the four bedrooms — Abby's room, Rose's room, Mama and Pop's room, and the baby's room.

Abby walked slowly into her room and across to the window. She stood with her eyes closed, then finally opened them and found herself staring at the side of the Burleys' house and an upstairs window. It was a very nice house and window. But it wasn't the ocean.

Abby sighed. She bounced once on her new bed, trailed her fingers across her new vanity, sat briefly in her new rocking chair, and peeked into the empty closet.

Rose appeared in the hallway. "Let's see if we're allowed to walk into town by ourselves," she said.

"All right. But we can't ask until we've unpacked." Abby knew Mama wouldn't want her and Rose to have a treat until they'd fulfilled their duties. More important, Abby felt she couldn't leave her strange new room until she had made it her own.

Mama balked when Abby and Rose asked to walk into town without a grown-up.

"It's only two blocks," Abby protested.

"Children aren't safe anymore," said Mama, and Abby thought of the newspaper headline she'd seen the other day: *Lindbergh Baby Found Slain*. The baby, the son of the famous aviator Charles Lindbergh, had been kidnapped from his crib in the middle of the night on March 1st. On May 12th, the baby had been found not far from his home in New Jersey — dead. Someone had killed him. Mama had wept when she'd heard the news. And she'd said that children weren't safe anymore, not even in their own beds. She had said that many times in the past few days, occasionally adding, "What is the world coming to?"

"But can't we just walk into town?" Abby asked again. "We aren't babies. And we know where we're going. Anyway, starting tomorrow we're going to be walking to school by ourselves."

Mama finally relented, but only after Pop said, "We can't coddle them forever, Nell."

"Thank you!" Abby and Rose cried before Mama could change her mind. They ran across their front lawn, stopping briefly to watch Mike, who was replanting the rosebushes, and who kept his eyes on his work.

"Do you know the way into town?" Rose asked Abby as they passed the Burleys' house.

"Of course. Right up there is the main street," Abby said, pointing. "The one with all the stores —"

"Let's go to the drugstore," Rose interrupted, "and get ice cream."

"Let's look around a little first. Gosh, I can't believe we live in town now. And that we can just walk right to the drugstore or the toy store or the library whenever we want. We'll walk into town every single day on our way to school and back."

Abby took Rose's hand and they turned on to the main street, and before them lay the market and the movie theatre and the hardware store and the toy store. Gulls called above their heads and landed on the roofs of the stores, standing in important lines. Men left their jobs as clerks and bankers and waited impatiently for sandwiches and bowls of soup at the counter in Griswold's. Ladies hurried in and out of Treat's with their packages of meat and bags of flour.

"No more Hammer's," said Abby happily. "No more 'Don't touch, little girl!'"

Abby and Rose peeked into the library and Abby asked the librarian if *Nancy's Mysterious Letter* was in. "Due back tomorrow" was the reply, and Abby realized she could stop in again on her way home from school the next day.

Later, Abby and Rose, full of strawberry ice cream from the counter at the drugstore, walked to their new home with sticky hands. They turned onto Haddon and Abby studied the houses they passed. The first one was tall, painted white, with black shutters. Sitting on what Pop had told her was called a veranda were an old man and an old woman, who both seemed to be asleep. But as Abby and Rose hurried by the house, the woman suddenly opened her eyes, leaned forward in her rocking chair, and called, "Where are your manners? Didn't anyone ever teach you to address your elders?"

Rose looked helplessly at Abby, and Abby said timidly, "Good afternoon." Then she added, "My name is Abby Nichols and this is my sister, Rose. We just moved here."

"I know who you are!" yelled the woman.

"Shouldn't you tell us *your* names?" asked Rose.

Abby looked at her sister in horror, but the woman began to laugh. She settled back in her chair and said, "I certainly should. I'm Mrs. Evans, and that's Mr. Evans taking his nap."

"We're going to have a baby soon" was Rose's reply. "Babies nap all the —"

"Well, it was nice meeting you!" said Abby loudly. "We have to get home now. Come on, Rose."

Abby hustled her sister along Haddon. "You can't say things like that to grown-ups!" she whispered loudly.

At the next house, a baby carriage was parked in the middle of the front lawn, and in it was a fat baby wearing a white bonnet. Curled up on a blanket at the baby's feet was an orange kitten. A little girl and a little boy tossed a ball back and forth, but they stopped and stared when they saw Abby and Rose.

"Hello!" called Abby, and the girl waved solemnly at her.

At the house next to that one, Abby paused and gazed up at the windows and the turrets and the fancy wooden decorations over the porch and under the eaves. Mama called them gingerbread.

"You know who lives there?" Abby asked Rose.

"The Burleys."

"*Zander* Burley," said Abby.

"Who's he?"

"That boy in seventh grade. The one who's always reading and always writing and always winning awards."

"You mean me?"

Abby whirled around and behind her stood Zander Burley, tall and lanky and perfectly handsome, his round glasses sliding down his nose. He grinned at Abby, who was blushing deeply.

"You should look before you speak," he added.

"I —" said Abby. "I —"

"So I guess you're the new neighbors," said Zander. "Well, see you." He strode up the walk to his house and let himself inside, the screen door slamming behind him.

"He thinks he's so great," muttered Abby, and strode into her own house.

When darkness fell that night, Abby closed the door to her room, turned off her light, and knelt on the window seat. Framed in her own window was a bedroom window at the Burleys'. And in the middle of the window was Zander, sitting at a desk, books piled beside him, writing furiously on a tablet. He wrote with a pencil and every now and then he paused to lick the point. Abby stared at him for a while, then drew her curtains, crept off of the window seat, changed into her nightgown, and slid under the blankets on her new bed.

She listened for a long time and thought maybe she could hear the faintest whisper of the ocean, but she wasn't sure. The wind rustled the branches of the pine trees behind the house and the damp air swept her hair back from her face. She rolled from side to side. A whole big bed all to herself. A whole big bed, and no Rose breathing heavily beside her or wrapping her cold feet around Abby's legs.

The door to her room opened then, and silhouetted in the light from the hallway was her sister.

Abby said nothing.

Rose said nothing.

Before Abby knew it, Rose had tiptoed across the room and curled against her sister's back, and they slept like kittens until the sun rose.

Chapter 6

"Fred, Fred, Freddy . , . Fred?"

Abby crossed her arms and leaned against Fred's crib, staring down at the baby. He gazed solemnly back at her. She raised his shirt and tickled his belly. He made a face and kicked his legs.

"Won't you smile at me?" Abby asked her brother. "Please? Just one smile?"

Fred rolled his eyes to the side.

Abby thought Fred's head looked a little too large for his body. And that it was lopsided. Maybe. If she looked at his head from one direction, it seemed okay, but when she looked straight down at him, she could see the faint bulge on the left side. She knew her parents saw it, too, but they didn't like to talk about it. Mama kept taking Fred to Dr. Rainey, though. And Abby had heard her discussing Fred with Sheila, the baby nurse.

"Shouldn't he be sitting up by now?" Mama had asked Sheila more than once. "Abby was crawling by the time she was nine months old. And Rose had already said her first word at this age. But Fred can't even hold himself up."

Fred wasn't sitting up or crawling or talking. He didn't hold on to his bottle either, and he showed absolutely no interest in rattles or his teddy bear or games of peekaboo.

"I want to hear his voice," Rose had said one day to Mama, and Abby had seen tears in Mama's eyes because Fred didn't make a sound, except when he was crying, which was often.

Abby had turned on her sister. "Rose. He's a baby. He can't talk yet."

But Mama had replied, "Rose has a point. He should be babbling by now."

Fred was like a big doll. You could feed him and change him, but he didn't give much back.

Now Abby tried to sit Fred up in his crib. He slumped to the side and then slid all the way over until he was sprawled on his back again. Abby sighed and left him there. Sheila would come in and dress him for the party soon.

Abby, already wearing her new white dress, the one from Haworth's, ran downstairs to the dining room where she found Mama and Pop and Rose seated around the table, eating Ellen's scrambled eggs and muffins.

"Good morning, birthday girl," said Mama.

"Even though it isn't really your birthday," said Rose.

"Well, it will be soon enough," said Mama. "And look." She gestured through the open French doors. "Perfect weather for a beach picnic."

Abby smiled and took her place at the table. She wondered if she dared ask Pop one more time if she couldn't invite Orrin to her eleventh birthday party. The planning of the party, from beginning to end, had been a little like President Roosevelt trying to pass the programs in the New Deal, which Abby had been reading about in the newspaper. The New Deal sounded like a good idea to her, even though plenty of people opposed it, including Pop. Mr. Roosevelt wanted to get the nation back on its feet and out of the Great Depression, and he had all sorts of plans for doing that. But he had to bargain and fight and compromise every step of the way. And that was how the planning of the party had gone.

"What would you like to do for your birthday, Abby?" Pop had asked her several weeks earlier.

Abby, who had already given her birthday quite a bit of thought, had answered instantly, "Could I please have a party this year? A real party? With guests? And games in the yard?" Neither she nor Rose had ever had an actual birthday party. Sometimes Aunt Betty and Uncle Marshall and the cousins had come by for supper, but birthday parties with cake and ice cream and guests and games and presents were for wealthy children.

Abby had been surprised when Pop had said no, since he seemed to want to convince all of Barnegat Point that the Nicholses had plenty of money now. But it turned out that he simply had other ideas about Abby's first party, and he suggested a picnic at the beach. "For all our friends," he said. "I mean, your friends. And their parents. A fancy picnic with all the trimmings. Ellen will make a feast."

Abby had reluctantly agreed. It wasn't quite what she had imagined, but maybe the kids could wear hats and play games in the sand. She started her guest list. Sarah's name headed it. Pop added Sarah's parents to the list. Abby wrote down Orrin and his mother and father. Pop crossed off the Umhays (all of them) and replaced them with the Burleys.

Eventually, Abby let Pop and Ellen plan the party, which would be held on Saturday, because Sunday, her actual birthday, was the Lord's day. Ellen worked out the menu. Pop finished the guest list. And Mama took Abby and Rose to Haworth's for new dresses.

"Fancy ones!" Pop had called as they'd left for the store.

"How are we supposed to play games in lace dresses?" Abby had whined as they'd walked into town, and her mother had leaned over to straighten the blankets in Fred's carriage and pretended she hadn't heard her.

In Haworth's, Miss Amelia, who walked around all day long with a measuring tape around her neck and a mouthful of pins, had removed the pins long enough to say, "My, how you two girls have grown just since the last time you were in the store. Abby, you especially." She had eyed Abby's chest and Abby had ducked her head and blushed, and Mama had once again busied herself with Fred. "I think you can go with something a little more grown-up, Abby. We'll make the bust a bit fuller. . . ."

At this, Rose had burst into a fit of giggles and Mama had made her sit in a corner of the store until Miss Amelia had finished measuring Abby.

It was when they were leaving the store later, Abby red-faced but secretly pleased about her new measurements, that they had passed the Spinning Top, and Abby had come to a stop so fast that Mama had run Fred's carriage into the backs of her legs.

"Mama! Look!" Abby had cried. She pointed to the store window. "That wasn't there yesterday. Oh, she's beautiful."

In the very center of the Spinning Top's window stood the loveliest doll Abby had ever seen. She was ten inches tall, and clearly the kind of doll that was just for looking at, not for playing with.

"She's a fairy queen," Rose had said, in awe.

Abby had studied every inch of the doll. She was wearing a white dress with panels of lace trimmed in gold, and fastened to her back were wings of white feathers, also trimmed in gold. On her head was a gold crown, and her golden hair fell in curls to her shoulders. Her mouth had been painted in a tiny, knowing smile.

"Mama," Abby had whispered, "that's what I want for my birthday. Could I have her? Please?" Abby couldn't see a price tag, but she figured Pop could afford her.

To Mama's credit, she didn't say, "Aren't you a little old for dolls?" Maybe that was because Mama understood that this wasn't just a doll; this was something beautiful to be treasured and admired and loved every day, even when Abby was a grown-up.

Mama had given Abby a small smile. "We'll see," she'd said, and they'd walked along silently, Abby picturing the fairy-queen doll until they'd turned onto Haddon and Fred had begun to cry.

*   *   *

So many people had been invited to Abby's birthday beach picnic, and Ellen had prepared so many dishes, that Mike had to drive two carloads of food, plates, glasses, and silverware to the beach beforehand. Pop and Ellen went along with the first load and stayed on the beach to watch over things. After the second load, Mike returned to the house for Mama, Abby, Rose, Fred, and Sheila.

Abby felt glamorous in her new dress with the fuller bust — which she knew Rose secretly envied — and she rode primly through town to the section of beach that Pop had declared was the perfect spot for a party. But once Mike had parked the car and Abby caught sight of Sarah and of her cousins and aunt and uncle, she couldn't help running like a kid across the sand and opening the box that she knew contained party hats. She handed a tiara to Sarah and a straw hat with a bird on it to Rose and stuck a crown on Fred's head as he lay in Sheila's lap. She reached into the box once more, pulled out a cowboy hat, spun around, and found herself facing Zander Burley.

Zander peered at her owlishly.

"Um, I guess you don't want a hat," said Abby.

"I —" He hesitated, then thrust his hand into his pocket and held out a small box. "This is for you."

"Really? For me?" Abby's hands began to shake, and

she clasped them behind her back, out of Zander's sight. This boy, the one she gazed upon most nights, wanting to know everything about him, had apparently noticed her, too. And he had brought her a present. "Should I open it?" she asked.

"Well, eventually."

Abby reached for the box and dropped the hat.

They both bent to pick up the hat and their heads knocked together. Zander laughed and Abby blushed.

"I'll just put the box over there," said Zander, and placed it on a blanket where a pile of small parcels was growing. Then he strode away to join a group of boys who Abby guessed must be the sons of people who worked for Pop.

"Abby!" Rose called then. "Let's play blindman's bluff!"

Abby was gathering her friends — the ones she actually knew — when she heard Fred begin to cry. She looked up for an instant, and was startled to see a figure standing beyond the rocks at the edge of the beach.

Orrin.

What was Orrin doing in Barnegat Point? Abby wondered, and at that moment Sarah tugged her elbow and said, "Abby! Look! Orrin's here. Did you invite him?"

Once again, Abby's cheeks burned. She shook her head. "Pop . . . well, you know."

Sarah frowned.

But Abby began to smile. She waved to Orrin, then ran across the beach to the skinny figure who now towered over her, his white-blond hair glistening in the sun. "You came!" she said breathlessly. "I — Pop wouldn't let me send you an invitation."

Orrin nodded. "I figured." His ruddy cheeks flamed even redder.

"How did you know about the party?"

"I just heard."

"Well, I'm glad you're here."

"I won't stay, though. I just wanted to say happy birthday. I wanted to give you a present, too, only . . . well, it isn't anything special."

Orrin offered Abby a small paper bag, then stuffed his hands in his pockets and clambered back over the rocks.

Abby watched him for a moment. "Orrin!" she called. "Orrin!" Then, realizing how loud her voice was, she looked guiltily over her shoulder and spotted Pop on the beach. He was talking with Zander's father, his back to her.

"Orrin," Abby called again, but more softly, and Orrin didn't hear her. He had already disappeared beyond the rocks. She wanted to shout at Pop, to punish him for all his unfairness. Instead she looked at the spot where Orrin had been standing and then opened the bag. Inside was a piece of red sea glass, one of the rarest colors, tumbled as smooth and as soft as Fred's cheek. Abby had collected plenty of blue and green and white sea glass, but she had never found a piece that glowed like a warm coal.

"Abigail!"

Abby turned at the sound of Pop's voice and ran back to the party.

"What are you doing over there?" he asked, glancing toward the rocks. "It's time to eat."

Abby's guests were standing at tables laden with salads (she counted three different kinds) and rolls and chicken and lobster. There was a platter of cold roast beef, a plate of deviled eggs, and jugs of tea and lemonade. The adults were laughing and talking, sitting self-consciously with their plates of food on blankets that Mike had spread on the sand. Abby saw Rose and two of the Blue Harbor Lane kids sit directly in the sand, waving pieces of chicken in the air and giggling. She longed to join them, but the sea glass in her hand pulled her thoughts back to Orrin, and to the sight of him disappearing from her world.

"Aren't you going to eat? It's your birthday party." Abby jumped at the sound of Zander's voice, and he grinned at her. "Come on." He took her by the elbow and steered her toward the food. He handed her a plate and she took it gratefully, jamming Orrin's gift into a pocket of her dress.

It was later, when Abby was so full she thought she would burst and the guests were sitting lazily on the blankets, drunk with sunshine and heavy food, that Pop stood and clinked a fork against a glass.

"This is a very special day," he announced. Everyone stirred and shaded their eyes to peer at him. "We're celebrating my daughter's eleventh birthday. I thank you all for coming. And now, Abigail, will you join me?" He extended his arm to Abby, who was sitting between Rose and Sarah on a rumpled, sandy blanket.

Abby, butterflies beating their wings in her stomach, got to her feet, stumbling slightly, and stood next to Pop.

"In honor of the day, I would like to present you with this gift," Pop announced, sounding as if he were addressing the town council. He reached into his breast pocket and withdrew a long, thin box.

Abby held out her hand, but Pop pulled the box back, lifted the lid, and displayed the gift inside for the guests to see. From the sand below, Abby heard Rose draw her breath in sharply. "A watch," her sister said in awe.

The box was velvet, black velvet, and inside was indeed a watch with a narrow silver band and a delicate silver face.

"Oh, Pop," Abby whispered.

She heard her sister's voice again. "What about the doll?"

Abby shook her head at Rose.

"A grown-up gift for a grown-up girl," Pop continued. He beamed around the beach at the guests.

Abby bit her lip. "Thanks, Pop. It's perfect," she said, aware that all eyes were on her, and that the guests — most of them anyway — would be impressed by this extravagant gift from a man who appeared to know his daughter, but who really did not know her at all.

"Maybe you can buy the doll yourself," Rose said to Abby sadly, when the party was over and the sisters were home again, sitting on the porch, looking out at the street as the sun lowered in the sky. "Let's go into town right now. We'll see how much she costs. You can save your money. We'll *both* save our money. You can pay me back later."

But the doll was no longer in the window. "Somebody must have bought her," said Abby, biting her lip again. She was not going to cry in front of Rose.

After supper, which no one had any appetite for, Abby thanked Pop for the party and climbed the stairs to her room. She laid the watch on her dresser and knelt on the window seat for a while. Zander's room was dark. Abby sat dreaming and thinking and finally went to bed. She imagined the fairy queen posed on her shelf and at last she allowed the tears to come, but she wiped them away quickly when the door to her room opened.

"Abby?" It was Mama's soft voice. "Are you awake?"

"Yes."

"I have something for you."

Mama closed the door quickly, sat on Abby's bed, and placed the doll in her arms. "I know this is what you really wanted," she whispered.

"Mama!"

"Shh. We can't let Pop know. This is our secret."

"Can I tell Rose?"

"Yes. But promise me, not a word to your father. Find a good hiding place. Pop wouldn't like it if he knew I went behind his back. He had his heart set on the watch."

"But he just wanted to impress his friends," said Abby. "That's why he bought it."

"No," Mama replied gently. "He truly thought the watch was a special gift for a young girl. But he's . . . well, never mind." She kissed Abby's forehead. "Happy birthday," she said, and tiptoed out of the room.

Chapter 7

Abby sat at her desk, her troubling arithmetic homework before her. Every year through fifth grade, she had spread her homework on the kitchen table and worked there, with the noise of Rose and her mother, and later of Fred and Ellen and Sheila, dancing around her. But now Abby was in sixth grade, and starting on the very first day of school, she had carried her stack of books upstairs to her room each afternoon and worked self-consciously at her desk, aware that if she could just fly, she would be able to slip through her window, across to Zander's window, and inside to his room where he was sitting at his desk, working on his high school assignments.

She turned away from the page of fractions she was desperately trying to multiply and looked at the darkness beyond her window. Not even suppertime, and already Barnegat Point was consumed by the dark.

Downstairs the front door banged and Abby heard her mother call, "Hello, Luther!"

She heard no answer from her father, though, and that was not a good sign. Abby tiptoed across her room and crept into the hall, where she leaned over the railing and listened.

"I nearly killed myself," her father was saying. "Fell over Fred's carriage. What's it doing in the drive? It should be put away."

Sheila's soft answering voice: "That was my fault, Mr. Nichols. I left it there this afternoon. I'll go move it."

"Pop?" said Rose, and Abby leaned farther over the railing. "Can I please have twenty cents? I need to —"

"For Pete's sake, Rose. No. Every time I turn around you're asking for something."

"But this is for —"

"What did I just say? *No.*"

Abby hurried down the stairs and into the parlor. She saw her sister walking backward in the direction of the kitchen. Fred, whom Sheila had left hastily in an armchair, began to wail, and Mama stooped to pick him up.

"Stop!" ordered Pop. "Leave him there. You coddle him." He paused for a moment, frowning at Fred, who had tumbled sideways and now lay on his back like an overturned turtle, arms flailing and wails growing louder. "How old is Fred anyway?"

"One year and two months," Abby answered.

Pop spun around. "Was I speaking to you?" he asked.

Abby froze. "No, sir."

"He's fourteen months old," said Mama quietly.

"And he can't even sit up yet. Look at him. I thought you were taking him to Dr. Rainey again."

"I was. I mean, I did. This morning."

"And?"

Mama glanced first at Rose and then at Abby. Finally she said to Pop, "Nothing's changed."

"Well, that's apparent."

"He said some babies just do things on their own time."

"And some doctors don't know what they're talking about. Maybe if you and Sheila didn't do everything for him —"

"If we didn't do things for him, do you think he could do them himself? Do you think he's suddenly going to sit up? This isn't my fault, Luther," said Mama, her tone still measured.

"He's not normal" was Pop's reply, and Abby could see a purple vein bulge on his temple. She imagined his blood angrily surging through his body.

Mama picked up Fred and turned him away from Pop, rocking him in her arms until Sheila returned. Sheila began to carry Fred upstairs.

"Put him in his high chair," ordered Pop. "He's going to eat with us tonight."

"He's already had his supper, Mr. Nichols," said Sheila.

"And he can't sit in the high chair," added Rose from the kitchen doorway.

Abby skirted around her father and pulled Rose into the dining room. Fiercely she whispered, "Don't upset him."

"He's already upset."

"I mean it, Rose. Look at the mood he's in. Don't say a word during dinner, no matter what happens."

"What if he asks me a question?"

"Then answer it politely. That's it. Don't give him any reason to get mad at you."

"Okay."

Abby watched as Cherry, a maid Pop had recently hired to help Ellen, placed the last of the silverware on the table, then disappeared silently into the kitchen.

"Everyone to the table!" Pop shouted from the parlor.

Abby and Rose were already standing stiffly at their places, hands at their sides. Mama followed Pop into the dining room and set Fred in his high chair. He slid forward, under the tray, and Mama caught him quickly, just before he banged his head. She sat him up again . . . and Fred slid down again.

Mama turned to cast an appealing glance at Pop, who glared at her.

"Make him sit," said Pop.

"He can't."

"Make him."

"Abby, hold Fred for a minute, please." Abby reached for her brother, and Mama pushed through the swinging door into the kitchen. When she returned, she was carrying one of Ellen's aprons. She placed it around Fred's middle and fastened the ties behind the chair. Fred slid again, but not as far.

"All right," said Pop. He took his seat, and Mama, Abby, and Rose took theirs.

Pop stepped on a buzzer hidden under the rug at his feet, and a moment later Ellen entered the dining room with a platter of ham. Cherry followed her with a dish of green beans.

"Serve him, too," Pop said to Ellen, inclining his head toward Fred.

"Luther," said Mama softly, "you know he can't eat that."

"Serve him," Pop repeated.

Ellen glanced at Mama before placing a slice of ham on the small plate on Fred's tray. When Ellen and Cherry had left the room, Pop rose, furiously cut up the ham, and placed a fork in Fred's fist. The fork fell to the floor. Pop picked it up, put it back in Fred's hand, closed his own hand around Fred's, stabbed a piece of ham with the fork, and jabbed the fork at Fred's mouth.

"Luther!" cried Mama, and Fred's face crumpled as his tears began to fall.

"Eat, dammit," said Pop in a frighteningly quiet voice.

Rose turned wide eyes to Abby, and Abby shook her head, reminding her sister to remain silent.

Pop pulled the ham off the fork and stuffed it into Fred's mouth. Fred gagged and spit it out, eyes watering as he started another slow slide toward the floor.

Mama was on her feet. "He can't chew well yet."

"A *cow* can chew," said Pop.

"Well, Fred can't."

Pop yanked the ties of the apron tighter and then slammed his way back to his chair. He ate his meal savagely, ignoring Fred's cries. No one said a word. When their plates were empty, Pop looked up and down the table and said, "Abby, where's your dessert fork?"

Abby looked at her place setting. "I don't know."

"Did you eat your dinner with it?"

"No, sir."

Pop slammed his foot on the buzzer. When Ellen appeared, he said, "Tell Cherry she's fired. There's a fork missing. We don't appreciate it when our silverware disappears."

"Yes, Mr. Nichols."

Rose got timidly to her feet. "May I please be excused?" she asked.

When Pop only grunted, Abby asked to be excused, too. She took Rose's hand and they fled upstairs.

"What do you think happened?" Rose asked as they huddled on Abby's bed.

"It's one of his moods," Abby replied.

"That's all?"

"Maybe. I don't know. Just stay out of his way."

"But it's Friday. There's no school tomorrow. How are we going to stay out of his way?"

"Maybe Mike will drive us to Lewisport and we can visit Sarah and Orrin and everyone. We could stay for the whole day. I'll ask Mama later."

They heard footsteps on the stairs then, and Rose ran into her room. Abby jumped off of her bed, perched on her desk chair, picked up a pencil, and pretended to tackle her arithmetic again. The footsteps paused farther down the hall, then continued to Abby's room.

"Abby?" said Mama firmly. "Gather your things together. We're going to the beach cottage."

"What? Right now?"

"Yes. You and Rose and Fred and I. Uncle Marshall is on his way over. He'll drive us there. And he'll be here soon, so get ready quickly."

Abby shoved away from her desk. She tiptoed out into the hall and listened for sounds from below. Nothing. She peeked into her sister's room. "Did Mama tell you?" she asked.

Rose nodded, eyes brimming.

"Don't cry now. Just get ready. It's okay. It will be better this way. We'll be at the house all weekend."

"Pop's going to be awful sore."

"Well, we have to do what Mama says."

Abby returned to her room. She put her schoolbooks into a satchel and grabbed a pair of shoes and some clothes. She unfastened her watch and left it on her dresser. At the last moment she placed the fairy-queen doll in the satchel. Then she knelt for a moment on the window seat, hoping for a glimpse of Zander, but his window was dark.

"Abby?" called Mama from Fred's room.

"Coming." Abby stepped tentatively into the hall.

Rose was peeking out of her doorway. "Where's Pop?" she whispered.

"He's downstairs," replied Mama. "It's okay."

"I think I'd like to wait until Uncle Marshall is here before I go downstairs," said Rose.

"Me, too," said Abby.

"All right," Mama replied. She started down the staircase with Fred in her arms, then turned around and handed him up to Abby. She kissed his forehead. "I love you, baby boy."

Abby, holding Fred, sat on the top step next to Rose until they heard Uncle Marshall's car outside.

"Children!" called Mama, and Abby carried Fred downstairs, while Rose followed, holding both her satchel and Abby's.

Uncle Marshall let himself in the front door without knocking.

"Marshall," said Pop, striding into the hall. "This really isn't necessary. There was a misunderstanding, that's all." He offered Uncle Marshall a smile.

Uncle Marshall stared stonily at Pop. Then he turned to Mama. "Go on, Nell. Take the children to the car. I'll be right there."

Abby hurried past her father and into the night, Fred on her hip, Rose at her heels.

"Good-bye! Have fun!" called Pop gaily from the front door as if his family were leaving on a vacation.

Uncle Marshall shoved the door closed with his foot then, and Abby couldn't hear anything else from inside. Not until she was sitting next to Rose in the back of Uncle Marshall's Ford Victoria, Mama cradling Fred in the front seat, did her hot tears begin to fall. She wept silently halfway to Lewisport.

The four of them stayed at the house on Blue Harbor Lane until Sunday evening, when Uncle Marshall drove them home again. It was the first time they had spent a weekend apart from Pop, but it wouldn't be the last.

Chapter 8

Pop drove down Blue Harbor Lane, whistling, his left elbow resting in the open window of the Buick. He was driving, Abby thought, just a little too fast.

"Pop, look out!" cried Rose, as Patches dashed across the road and ran under the Moresides' porch.

Pop slammed on the brakes and turned around to glare at Rose, who was sitting next to Abby in the backseat. "Do you want to get us all killed?" he exclaimed. "Don't say that unless something's going to run into us."

"But it was Sarah's cat, Pop. You almost hit him."

Pop didn't reply. He swiveled around, sped up, and made a fast turn into the drive by the beach cottage.

"Here we are!" said Mama gaily. "Everybody out." She opened her door, lifted Fred out of the car, and perched him on her hip.

Abby climbed out of the Buick and stood in the yard in front of the house. Before her spread the ocean. To the south, the beach swept away until the spit of land seemed to melt into the sky. To the north, it ended where the shore curved west and was swallowed by fir trees.

"Give your mother a hand, girls," said Pop, unloading boxes and suitcases from the car and piling them on the drive. "I'm going back to the house for a while. I'll see you later." He zoomed the Buick out of the drive and down the lane.

Abby watched him for a moment, then turned and took Fred from her mother.

"Just think," said Rose. "A whole month here."

Abby knew exactly what her sister meant. Their house in Barnegat Point was spacious and luxurious. But the beach cottage was better. It smelled of home. And it meant day after day after day of walking along the shore with Sarah and clamming with Orrin, of games of kick-the-can and cribbage. There would be evenings on the porch with Mama, watching the moon rise over the ocean, and afternoons of picking blueberries, to eat that night with cream. It didn't matter that they had to do all of their own cooking and chores. Not that Abby didn't like Ellen and Sheila and Mike, but she enjoyed having the little house just for her family.

Even better, Pop would be gone for days at a stretch. He planned to spend the first week of vacation at the cottage, but after that he was going to stay in Barnegat Point except on weekends.

"Come on, Fred," said Abby, hoisting her brother higher on her hip. "Come on, Freddy Fred. Do you want to see the water?"

Fred flashed Abby a drooly grin and waved his hands in front of his face.

"Can I take him to the beach?" Abby asked her mother.

"In a bit. Help me get everything inside first."

Abby carried Fred to the porch and was about to open the door, anticipating the first lungful of beach-house air that smelled of salt and woodsmoke and pine beams, no matter how long the house had been closed up. But before she opened the door, she heard Sarah call her name.

Abby turned around. "Sarah!"

Sarah ran across Abby's yard and hugged her and Fred at the same time. She had to reach down to do so. When sixth grade had started, Sarah had been the shrimp of the class. By the end of the year she was taller than most of the boys. And she was chestier than Abby — her mother had needed to take her to Haworth's in Barnegat Point so Miss Amelia could fit her for an adult brassiere.

The changes didn't matter, though. Sarah was Sarah, and when she and Abby were together, Abby felt as comfortable with her old friend as she had when they were three or six or ten.

"I can't believe you're here for a month," said Sarah.

"Want to see something?" asked Abby.

She set Fred on the floor and held her hand out to him. Fred reached for it and hauled himself to his feet.

"He can stand up!" exclaimed Sarah.

"He just learned how. And he's not even two yet, so that isn't really so slow." Abby chose not to think about Dr. Rainey's most recent diagnosis for Fred: *feebleminded and crippled*. How crippled could he be if he was standing up?

After lunch Mama took a nap when Fred did, resting on the porch with him nestled against her. Rose took off down Blue Harbor Lane in search of friends, and Abby and Sarah walked hand in hand along the beach, dashing in and out of the water, which was still icily cold.

"Did you hear about Liddie Kestler?" asked Sarah.

"No. What?"

"She likes Duncan."

"Duncan *Field*?"

"Yuh."

"But Duncan hates girls."

"I don't think so. He doesn't hate Liddie anyway."

Abby looked sideways at Sarah. "Who do you like?"

"*Me?* I don't like anyone. We're too young to like boys."

"We're exactly the same age as Liddie. Come on. Tell the truth. You like Orrin."

"Well, so do you."

"Just as a friend," said Abby, although she wasn't sure about this.

"Me, too. But if we both liked him as a boy," said Sarah, "then I would let you have him, because I think a best friend is more important than a boyfriend."

"Oh, so do I!" exclaimed Abby. "I wouldn't trade you for ten boys."

"When we grow up," said Sarah, "we should tell our husbands that we have to live next door to each other so that we can see each other every single day and our children can be best friends, too."

"Hey, look," said Abby. "There's Orrin. Orrin!" she called. "Orrin!"

Orrin was trudging barefoot along Blue Harbor Lane. He had, Abby decided, the skinniest legs she'd ever seen on a twelve-year-old boy.

"Where's your bucket?" asked Sarah.

"Don't need it. I'm looking for work," Orrin replied. The

sun beat down on his head, turning his blond hair as white as beach sand.

"You mean for a real job?" said Abby.

"I got to. Ma and Pap aren't working. It's up to me."

"What kind of work?" asked Sarah.

"Whatever anyone wants to give me. Nothing I can't do. Well, almost nothing. I can paint stuff or collect stuff or repair stuff or haul stuff."

"You are good at all those things," said Sarah loyally.

"Are your parents out looking for work, too?" asked Abby.

"Nawp," said Orrin after a moment. "They're asleep. They're — Hey, what's that?"

"What's what?" asked Abby.

"That." Orrin pointed across the lane and behind the row of houses. "That shiny thing back there."

Abby shaded her eyes. "Don't know."

"Come on," said Orrin. "Let's go see. Shouldn't be anything back there."

Orrin and Abby ran across the road and between Abby's cottage and the Becketts', Sarah trailing behind, until they reached the track that ran behind the Blue Harbor houses.

"Wow," said Orrin under his breath as he stopped short by a gleaming red-and-white car. "A Chrysler Sport Coupe.

She's not brand-new — I think she's a year or two old — but she's a beauty." He ran his hand along the door, the spoked wheels, the headlamps. "I'd give anything for a car like this." He paused. "I'd give anything for a car of any kind."

"What's it doing back here?" asked Sarah. "Orrin, you'd better stop touching it. The owner won't like it."

"Well, the owner isn't here. Whoever he is. Besides, I'm not doing anything."

Abby glanced up and down the track and then at the backs of the houses. No one was in sight. "Let's sit in it," she said. "This is the fanciest car I've ever seen."

"No!" said Sarah. "You'd better not. Why do you want to sit in it?"

Abby looked at Orrin. "I just do. You do, too, don't you, Orrin?"

Sarah backed up a few paces, but Orrin jumped behind the wheel of the car and Abby climbed in on the other side.

"I feel like a rich person," said Orrin, grinning.

"Sarah, come on!" called Abby. "There's room for you."

Sarah shook her head, cheeks pink. "You don't know who it belongs to. What if you get caught?"

"Well, no one's around but us," Orrin pointed out. He placed his hands on the steering wheel and twisted it. "Look at me in my fancy car. Just out for a drive. Driving along, waving to girls and rich people. Tonight I'm going to have steak for supper because I'm so rich. . . . Sarah, come *on*."

"Yeah, why are you being such a baby?" said Abby. "You're ruining everything."

"What am I ruining?" asked Sarah. Abby heard a tremor in her voice, but ignored it.

"You're like a teacher," said Orrin.

"You're a scaredy-cat," said Abby.

Sarah said nothing and Abby felt treacherous, but couldn't stop herself because Orrin was next to her and the car was dangerous and beautiful, and the sun was shining, and it was the first day of her vacation.

"Scaredy-cat," Abby repeated, and the next thing she knew, Sarah was climbing into the car, wedging herself between Abby and the door.

"All right," said Orrin. "That's better." He twisted the steering wheel again, and bounced up and down in his seat. Then Abby bounced up and down in her seat until the car was shaking, and the next thing any of them knew, the Chrysler had started to roll forward.

"Hey!" shrieked Sarah. "Stop! Make it stop!"

"Get out now!" cried Abby.

The car had been parked at the top of a slope, a slope so slight, it was hardly even noticeable. But the car gathered speed and Sarah couldn't figure out how to open her door and Orrin was concentrating on steering so that they wouldn't hit a tree.

"Stop, stop, stop!" Sarah shouted.

"I can't get the brake to work!" Orrin shouted back.

"Open your *door*!" Abby yelled at Sarah. "Orrin, open yours!"

The Chrysler hurtled forward, crashing through bushes and scraping against rocks. Abby began to scream and just when she was thinking of climbing over Sarah and jumping out of the car, she saw two things directly ahead: a fir tree and Pop.

Pop's mouth had opened into a shocked O. He jumped out of the path of the car and waved his arm to their left.

"Steer that way!" cried Abby. "Turn left, Orrin!"

Orrin jerked the wheel to the left and the car rumbled off the track and around Pop and the tree. Orrin stomped furiously on the brake and at last the car came to rest in a rocky field.

Pop was at Orrin's door in an instant. He yanked it open and jerked Orrin out of the car. "What do you think you're doing? I should throttle you!"

"Pop!" shouted Abby, leaping out of the car after Orrin. "Pop, stop! It wasn't his fault."

"He was driving my car, wasn't he? Who else's fault could it be?"

"*Your* car?" said Abby as Sarah finally wrenched her own door open and tumbled to the ground.

"Yes, my car. I just bought it. It needs repairs. I was going to work on it here on the weekends. But that's not the point. You three could have gotten yourselves killed. Not to mention that you've wrecked an expensive car." Pop walked all around the Chrysler, running his hands over dents and scratches, a broken headlamp.

"Pop, we didn't mean any —"

Pop held up his hand and Abby fell silent. "Abigail, you are forbidden to see Orrin and Sarah."

"What? Ever? But they're my — I mean, Sarah is my best friend. Besides, this didn't have anything to do with her. She didn't want to get in the car. She even told Orrin and me *not* to get in."

"Go home, then, Sarah," said Pop, and Sarah turned and fled. Pop glared at Orrin. "You're a bad influence. I don't want you in my house or in my yard or anywhere near my daughter again. Do you understand?"

Orrin crossed one bare foot over the other and stared at the ground.

"Orrin?" said Pop in the quiet voice that Abby found much more frightening than his shouting.

"Sorry," whispered Orrin.

"I asked if you understood me."

"Yuh."

"Then you go home, too. I'd ask you to pay for the damages, but I know you can't."

Abby saw Orrin flinch. "Maybe you could let Orrin work in your shop until —" she started to say.

"Out of the question," said Pop. "I know what kind of workers his people are. Let him stew. Let him think about what he's done and the fact that he can't make it right. Go, Orrin."

Orrin turned wounded eyes to Abby. She started to reach for his hand but drew back in a hurry. "Sorry," she whispered as Orrin, keeping his eyes now on the track, began the walk back to Blue Harbor Lane.

Abby looked from her father to the damaged car. "I'll help pay to have it fixed. I'll do —"

"We'll discuss it later," said Pop. "Just stay away from Orrin Umhay."

Chapter 9

Friday, February 15th, 1935

Abby could hear the cries before she was fully awake, before she realized they were a newborn's cries and not Fred's. She leaped out of bed, pulled on her dressing gown, and collided with Rose in the hallway.

"Doesn't that baby ever stop crying?" demanded Rose crossly.

"Babies are babies," Abby replied sensibly. "Adele doesn't cry any more than Fred did."

"Well, she's louder."

"Go back to sleep."

"I can't. She's too noisy. Anyway, I'll just have to get up in fifteen minutes to get ready for school." Rose studied her sister. "Are you going to school today?"

"I don't think so. Mama needs me. I'll go back on Monday."

"But Ellen and Sheila are here to help Mama."

"She needs *me*," Abby said. "So does Fred. It's just for one more day." She lowered her voice. "You saw Mama last night. She should be happy. She has a new baby. But something's not right. She didn't cry this much after Fred was born."

"I know," said Rose, and ducked back in her bedroom.

Abby tiptoed down the hall to her parents' room and peeked inside. Her mother was leaning against two large pillows, Adele cradled to her chest, and she was crying softly while Adele wailed. Abby looked at them in alarm.

"What's the matter?" she asked. She glanced around the room and wondered where her father was.

"She won't feed," Mama sobbed. "She just won't. And then she cries because she's hungry. Why won't she feed?"

Abby remembered Mama on the day after Fred had been born, complaining that he wouldn't feed, and she felt as if someone had stabbed her with an icicle. This couldn't possibly be happening again. "Oh, I'm sure —" she started to say. She had been about to say that she was sure Adele wasn't going to be anything like Fred, but how could she be sure of that? Instead she said, "I'm sure she'll feed when she gets really hungry."

"She's really hungry now," Mama replied quietly.

"Just try a little longer." Abby sat on the bed and put her arm around her mother. "Maybe if you stop crying, she'll calm down. Remember when Rose and I were little and you would sing 'My Bonnie' to us?"

Mama nodded and leaned into Abby. Abby began to sing, "My bonnie lies over the ocean. My bonnie lies over the sea. My bonnie lies over the ocean. . . ."

"Now Fred's crying," said Mama a moment later.

"But Adele is feeding," Abby whispered. She got silently to her feet, not daring to move the bed for fear of disturbing her new little sister. "I'll go get Fred. Don't worry about anything."

Abby hurried down the hall just as Sheila appeared at the top of the stairs. "Adele's feeding," Abby reported. "I'll take care of Fred."

"There won't be anything left for me to do," said Sheila. She patted Abby's arm. "You're a good little mother."

"Where's Pop?" asked Abby, pausing outside Fred's room.

"Gone to work."

"Already? Rose hasn't even left for school."

Sheila shrugged, and Abby turned her attention to Fred's soggy diaper. "He's never here," she said to her brother. "He's very good at disappearing." Then, realizing that she was holding Fred's legs far too tightly, she leaned over and kissed his forehead. "Sorry. Sorry, Fred."

*   *   *

The day was dreary, dreary in the way only the middle of February can be. The sky was pale gray, and a cold rain pounded the two inches of snow that had fallen the previous day. Abby had hoped the snow might be a good omen. Purity, a new start. A Valentine's Day snowfall for a Valentine's Day baby. But Mama's delivery of Adele had been difficult — twice the doctor had been called to the house. And then there were Mama's tears, which never seemed to stop flowing. But yesterday was yesterday, and today was today, and Mama was finally asleep, and now that Adele's tummy was full, she was asleep, too.

Late that morning Abby and Fred sat in the window seat in the parlor, and Abby gazed outside at the dim, dark morning. The snow had already turned as gray as the sky, and the rain was washing ragged rivulets of slush into the street.

"Ba?" said Fred, holding a block aloft.

"Yes! Block!" Abby cried. "Good boy!"

"Hoo?" asked Fred, holding a different block aloft.

Abby stared at him. "Block," she said again finally. "It's a block, Fred."

"Abby?" called Ellen from the kitchen. "Are you and Fred ready for lunch?"

"Is Pop coming home?"

"For lunch? I don't think so."

"He should be here with his new baby," muttered Abby, but not so loudly that Ellen could hear her. At the same time she realized that she was relieved not to have to see Pop until dinnertime. Everyone else in the household probably felt the same way.

"We'll eat in a little while," said Abby. "Thanks." Her mind wandered to the subject of the mail and what might arrive in it that day. She was hoping for a letter from Orrin, but Orrin, partly because he didn't have much use for reading or writing, and partly, Abby supposed, because he was a boy, wrote to her only every few weeks or so. Once, over a month had passed between his letters, even though Abby wrote to him several times a week.

Three years earlier, Abby had worried that their friendship would suffer when she moved to Barnegat Point, but at least back then she and Orrin could still see each other in school. Now, however, the Umhays lived fifty miles north of Barnegat Point. They had moved suddenly the previous August, just before Abby and Sarah and Orrin were to begin seventh grade. This was all the more wrenching since Abby hadn't found out about it until the Umhays had been gone for two days. She hadn't been able to say good-bye to Orrin, and if he hadn't thought to mail her a letter early in September (he sent it to Sarah's house so Pop wouldn't see it) she might never have known where he was. The only good thing about the Umhays' flight (Abby suspected that Orrin's father had run into a little trouble with the law) was that Pop's punishment no longer held any water. Abby couldn't see Orrin even if she wanted to.

But the letters had to remain a secret.

At exactly three o'clock that afternoon, the front door burst open and Rose clattered into the front hall, followed by Sarah.

"Sarah wants to meet the baby!" Rose announced.

"If that's okay," Sarah added, sounding apologetic. She stood uncertainly by the door, cradling her books and leaning forward slightly. Abby knew she was listening for Pop. "Only if it's okay," she repeated. "My mother's in town and she said I could visit you until she's finished with her shopping."

"Actually," said Abby, "I think it might be better if you saw the baby another time. Mama isn't . . . I think she's asleep."

"I understand," said Sarah. She glanced upstairs. "Is Adele cute?"

"She's all red and wrinkled like an old plum," Rose replied. "An old red plum with hair."

Sarah laughed. "She'll get better."

"I hope so," said Rose, "because she looks pretty awful right now."

"Maybe you could visit her on Monday," Abby suggested.

Sarah nodded. "Well . . . I'll just go, then."

"Wait," said Abby. "We'll come with you. Fred and I have been stuck indoors all day, but look — the sun's coming out. Let's put Fred in his carriage and we'll all walk into town. You can meet your mother there."

Abby had just bundled Fred into his jacket, mittens, and hat when the doorbell rang.

"I'll get it," said Abby. She opened the front door to find old Mrs. Evans, from down the street, holding a basket covered with a checked dishcloth, Mr. Evans hovering behind her.

Mrs. Evans smiled broadly. "I heard the stork visited your house."

"That's true," said Abby proudly. "He brought a little girl. Her name is Adele."

"She looks like a plum!" called Rose from the hall.

"Well, we just thought we'd drop by and leave you this pie. Goodness, it seems like only yesterday that Fred was born." Mrs. Evans leaned into the hall. "Where *is* Fred? How's he getting on?"

"Oh, he's fine," said Abby. She stepped forward, inching Mrs. Evans back onto the porch. "We're just about to take a walk."

Mrs. Evans glanced at the carriage, which was parked at the bottom of the porch steps. "He's getting a little big to ride in a carriage, isn't he?"

He was. But eight months had passed since Fred had first stood up, and he was no closer to walking than before. And since he was getting too big for Abby to carry, she had no choice but to wheel him around in the carriage.

"Thank you so much for the pie, Mrs. Evans," said Abby. "Thanks, Mr. Evans. I'll let Mama know you stopped by."

She closed the door, whisked the pie into the kitchen, and handed it to Ellen, saying, "This is from Mrs. Evans. We're going for a walk. We'll take Fred with us."

"All right, Little Mother."

Outside, Abby heaved Fred into the carriage and she, Rose, and Sarah set off for town.

"I wish we didn't have to walk by the Evanses' house every day," whispered Rose. "They look out their windows and stare at Fred. So do half the people on the street."

"Well, don't pay any attention," Abby replied. "They're busybodies, all of them."

In town, Abby bought suckers for Rose and Fred, and she and Sarah looked in the window of Clayton's, which had a display of ladies' hats.

"If you could buy any of those hats, which one would it be?" Sarah asked.

"That one," said Rose instantly, pointing to a straw hat with an alarming collection of flowers and birds around the rim.

"What about you, Abby?"

Abby shrugged. "I don't know."

"Come on. Just choose one."

"I can't."

Sarah scrutinized Abby. "You look awful tired," she said, as Rose ran ahead to the toy store.

Abby shrugged again.

"You don't have to do everything yourself, you know. That's what Sheila and Ellen are there for. You should be back in school."

"You don't know what it's like, Sarah," said Abby quietly.

"Sorry. I — Never mind. I didn't mean anything by it." Sarah reached for her friend's hand and squeezed it. Abby squeezed back.

Then Fred dropped his sucker and began to cry, and Abby said, "We'd better get on home. I'll see you on Monday,

Sarah, okay?" And Abby and Rose took turns pushing the very heavy carriage back to Haddon Road.

They were just passing the Evanses' house, Rose making gruesome faces in case they were spying out their windows, when Abby felt someone take her elbow, and she turned to find Zander Burley, his arm now linked with hers.

"Happy Valentine's Day," he said, "one day late." He withdrew his arm and loped ahead of Abby and Rose, along the sidewalk and across the lawn to his front door. Abby watched him, thinking that he moved very gracefully for a boy, and noticing that his jaw had grown squarer and his shoulders broader.

"Abby has a boyfriend!" Rose chanted when Zander was out of earshot.

"No, I don't."

Later, after Abby had lugged Fred back inside and was taking off his jacket, she heard a crinkling sound and reached into the pocket of her coat. Her hand closed around an envelope. She pulled it out and saw her name in neat printing. ABIGAIL.

She waited until she was alone in her room to open it, and inside she found a card showing a girl and boy joyfully riding a giant bumblebee, the words *Valentine, I'm abuzz over you* trailing in the wake of the bee. She flipped the card open.

Zander had written BEE MINE, ZANDER in the same neat handwriting.

Abby frowned, then smiled, and added the card to the ones she'd received from Rose and Sarah the day before.

She hadn't dared to give Zander a Valentine.

Chapter 10

Saturday, December 21st, 1935

"It snowed!" Rose announced. "Abby, it snowed last night!"

Abby sat up fast, tossing her covers back, and knelt on her window seat. Snow covered the ground and the branches of the trees and the roof of Zander's house.

"Ha!" said Rose from the doorway. "You're using the snow as an excuse to look in Zander's window."

"I am not," said Abby, which was a lie. She liked any excuse at all to see what might be going on in Zander's room. Sometimes she watched him writing at his desk and some-times she watched him lifting weights, which he did because his older brothers told him he was as scrawny as a chicken. This was absolutely untrue. But sometimes, like now, the blind was drawn, and then Abby felt unreasonably shut out and disappointed.

"His blind is down," she said, and flopped back on her bed.

Rose hesitated in the doorway. "Mama's talking about the babies again," she whispered.

"What?"

"The babies. The ones God took."

Abby sighed. "I don't know what to do about that."

"Why can't she be satisfied with her living children?" asked Rose, twisting the end of one braid around her finger. "She has us, and she has Fred, and she has Adele, who actually *is* a baby. But she's been outside, covering up the rosebushes and wondering why God took her babies. Pop saw her and yanked her arm and said, 'Go in the house, the neighbors are watching,' because Mama was only wearing her nightie and a pair of boots."

Abby closed her eyes briefly and Rose sat on the end of her bed. "Don't worry. Sheila's taking care of Fred and Adele," said Rose cautiously, trying to gauge her sister's mood.

"It's almost Christmas. I thought the holidays would make Mama feel better."

"So did I," Rose replied.

"Maybe . . . I don't know."

"I wanted to make gingerbread today."

"Ellen will help you."

"I wanted to make gingerbread with Mama."

Abby gave her sister a small smile. "Sarah's coming over later. Her parents are going to do some Christmas shopping in town. Maybe Sarah and I will go into town, too. Want to come with us?"

Rose nodded. "Okay. Thanks."

Sarah arrived just before lunch. "Bye, Mother. Bye, Dad," she called as the Moresides waved from the windows of their car.

"How long can you stay?" Abby asked her.

"Mother said they'll be busy for three or four hours. Let's go play with the baby first. Please? Can I hold her?"

"In a bit," said Abby. "She's napping now."

"You're so lucky to have a brother and sisters."

"Yeah," said Rose, "but at your house on Christmas morning, you get all the presents."

"Rose?" called Pop's voice from the parlor. "That sounded greedy."

Rose looked at the floor. "Sorry, Pop," she replied.

Lunch was chicken soup and cinnamon toast served at the kitchen table, Fred kicking his heels noisily against his high chair. Abby's parents ate in the dining room, much to the girls' relief.

"Done!" Rose cried suddenly, drinking the last swallow of soup directly from her bowl. She cast a nervous glance toward the dining room. "Let's go now."

"Where are we going?" asked Sarah.

"Into town?" Abby suggested.

"Let's play in the snow first," said Rose. "We've hardly had any snow so far."

This was true. Except for a surprise snowfall in the middle of October, the autumn had been unusually mild.

"What do *you* want to do?" Abby asked Sarah.

Sarah screwed up her face. "Take a walk?" she said finally.

"Take a walk?!" exclaimed Rose, dismayed. "You sound like the grown-ups." But when Abby and Sarah bundled up and left the house, she followed them.

Snow had started to fall again, and Abby and Sarah scuffed through it in their lace-up boots. "Are you going to walk with us or not?" Abby shouted, without turning around.

"How did you know I was here?" Rose called.

"You're noisy. Come on. Catch up."

"Are you going to talk about boys?"

Sarah laughed. "What boys?"

"Any boys."

"No. We're talking about what we want for Christmas."

"I want a dog," said Rose, hurrying to Abby's side.

"A sister," said Sarah.

"Poetry books," said Abby.

"You just want poetry books because Zander likes poetry," said Rose.

The girls emerged from a grove of fir trees at the western edge of town and found themselves at the top of a small hill.

"Look, there's Miller's Pond," said Sarah, pointing to the bottom of the hill. "Last one there's a rotten egg."

Sarah took off down the hill, slipping in the snow and laughing, her legs pumping faster and faster. Abby and Rose ran after her. At the bottom of the hill, Abby skidded to a stop, Rose running into her, but Sarah kept going and called breathlessly over her shoulder, "I'll bet the pond's frozen now!"

"No, it isn't!" Abby called back. "Not after one snowstorm! Sarah, stop!"

"Stop, stop!" shouted Rose.

But Sarah laughed and sped up, and when she reached the old, ragged stalks of cattails at the edge of the pond, she leaped through them, skidding across the fragile sheet of ice that had formed. Abby could see puddles of water around some of the cattails and she remembered the previous winter when she and Zander and Rose had stood at this same spot after school one day and watched a dog step curiously onto the snowy pond and fall through the ice. He'd made only a small splash and then had struggled and thrashed while

Abby and Zander had run to him. Zander had reached him first, just as the dog had heaved himself up the bank and bolted away, stopping to shake himself at the edge of the woods.

Sarah was far beyond the edge of the pond when Abby heard a low creaking sound, and then Sarah's feet disappeared, swallowed by the snow and ice and frigid water. Her coat billowed up around her waist like the parachutes Abby had seen in newsreels at the picture show.

"Sarah!" Rose shouted again. *"Sarah!"*

Abby ran to the cattails and placed one boot tentatively on the snow.

"No, Abby!" Rose called. "Don't go out there."

"She can't swim," said Abby. She set her foot more firmly on the snow and felt her boot fill with water. She pulled her foot out. Then she looked to Sarah — but Sarah wasn't there.

Rose whispered, "She's gone."

Abby stepped back and stared across the pond. She shaded her eyes from the glare of the snow and the milk-white sky. She heard nothing but the lapping of water under ice.

"Sarah?" she said tentatively.

Beside her, Rose began jumping up and down. "Sarah, Sarah, Sarah!"

Abby stepped onto the ice again, but Rose jerked her back. "Don't! You'll go under, too. The water's freezing. We have to get help."

"I can't leave her." Abby's breath came in short gasps and she felt her throat tighten. "Sarah!" she called again.

Rose was already running up the hill. "You stay right there, Abby, so we'll know where she went in the water. But *don't go in*. I'll be back as soon as I can."

Abby sank into the snow. Then she stood up and looked for a branch. She had read in storybooks about drowning children being pulled from ponds by grabbing on to branches held out to them by rescuers. But there was no sign of Sarah, no one for Abby to pull ashore. She sat in the snow again, waiting for Sarah to emerge, for Sarah to jump out of the water like the dog had, for Sarah to run laughing along the bank and say it was all a joke. After a time, there was a great commotion on the hill above and then a crowd of men, followed by several women and a group of gawking, fascinated children, came running down to the pond. Pop was with the men. When he saw Abby, he folded her in his arms and hugged her to his chest fiercely.

The people — later Abby could never say exactly who they were; they were just people — shouted and ran along the bank, and then other people arrived with blankets and a stretcher. After Abby and Rose had explained — tearfully and with lots of gesturing — everything that they knew, Pop took a look around and started to lead them back up the hill.

"I want to stay!" cried Abby.

"No," Pop replied quietly.

"I can't walk anymore," said Rose suddenly, and plopped down, sitting in the snow. Abby noticed that her sister had lost her hat.

Pop said nothing more, but picked Rose up and carried her through the woods and back to Haddon Road, Abby trailing behind. At the bottom of their street, he set Rose down and took Abby by the hand.

"Do Mr. and Mrs. Moreside know?" she whispered.

"Someone went to find them."

"But do they know?" Abby persisted.

And Rose said, "Is she dead?"

"I don't have the answers," said Pop, and his voice was gentle.

Abby didn't ask any more questions. She stepped dazedly along, between her father and Rose. They passed the Evanses', where Abby thought she could feel eyes peering from behind curtains, and eventually Zander's house, where Zander himself was standing on the porch, watching them solemnly.

"It wasn't our fault," Abby wanted to say. But she stared at the ground and watched her boots and Pop's boots, matched her stride to his, and she and Rose and Pop walked wordlessly into their house.

Mama met them at the door and said nothing, but she gathered Rose and Abby into her arms. Abby didn't know how everyone had heard about Sarah, but it was plain that the news had already traveled halfway around Barnegat Point. She leaned back to look at Mama and asked again, "Do Mr. and Mrs. Moreside know?"

Mama and Pop exchanged a glance.

"Yes, they know," Mama said after a moment.

"Have they found her yet?"

"I don't think so," said Mama.

"Then maybe she's still alive," said Rose.

No one answered her.

Sarah's funeral was held three days later, on Christmas Eve at the little church in Lewisport. The church was decorated for the Christmas service, garlands of pine branches and red bows along the aisle, the Nativity arranged outside by the front door. Abby, Rose, Mama, and Pop sat five pews behind Sarah's parents. Mrs. Moreside cried during the entire service. Mr. Moreside placed his arm across his wife's shoulders and stared straight ahead at the minister, from the time the service began until at last it was over. Then he didn't move until someone — Sarah's uncle? — touched him on the shoulder.

The Moresides walked down the aisle, followed by Sarah's grandparents and aunts and uncles and cousins. When Mrs. Moreside passed Abby's family, she turned and glared at them.

"It wasn't our fault," whispered Abby. "She was my best friend."

Mama took her hand and held it until the four of them had climbed into their car and were heading back to Barnegat Point.

Chapter 11

Tuesday, September 22nd, 1936

Sometimes when Abby walked, alone, through Barnegat Point to the high school, she imagined that the other girls, walking in pairs or in laughing, noisy groups, were talking about her.

"Remember Sarah, that girl from Lewisport who drowned in Miller's Pond? She was Abby Nichols's friend. Her *best* friend."

"Have you seen her brother? He's a cripple. He's four years old and he can't walk yet. My aunt said he's an idiot, too."

"Her mother's crazy. There's something wrong in that family."

"And her father is mean! He fired my father just for being late."

Abby longed for the days of walking to the grammar school with Rose and meeting up with Sarah and Orrin. At the beginning of eighth grade she and Sarah had felt like queens. The eighth graders were the most important students in the entire school. They could boss the younger kids around and brag about going to the high school the next year. The teachers gave them special privileges — they were allowed to walk into town at lunchtime if they had permission from their parents — and they were in charge of the Christmas program and the spring carnival. Then in June they got to have an actual graduation ceremony.

All during that autumn, Abby and Sarah had gleefully walked to the drugstore and eaten sandwiches at the soda fountain anytime Sarah had saved enough money to buy lunch. In December they'd been elected co-authors of the Christmas program and together had written a play about a lost lamb and a shepherd and how the star that shone in the sky on the night Jesus was born had cast enough light to help the shepherd find the lamb, which later grew up to save the shepherd's life. The play had been a big hit. Two days later Sarah had drowned and Abby, without a best friend, without Orrin, had crept through the remainder of the school year, a solitary, marked figure. She had become "the girl whose best friend drowned." Rose still walked to and from school with her, of course, and occasionally Zander tried to talk to her. But Abby felt as if she were wearing a sign that proclaimed her new sad status, and she didn't know how to erase the words on the sign.

What she remembered most about the next few months was the quiet. People tended to be quiet around her, and she was quiet in return. Her teachers were solicitous and forgiving. The other girls in her class spoke to her sweetly and slipped her apples and hard candies and little notes. Until they didn't anymore. Until they were more interested in seeing who got Valentine cards from boys, and in buying fabric to make dresses for the spring cotillion, and in being elected to the planning committee for the spring carnival.

Abby walked to school with Rose, sat silently in her classroom, came home, did her homework, then sat at her desk and wrote stories and poems and glued them into a scrapbook.

On graduation day she won three of the five academic awards: for composition, for history, and for overall highest grades. She smiled at the principal and thanked him politely, walked home with her family, and spent the summer reading and writing, taking care of Adele, and trying to teach Fred to walk. She found that she cared about little else, including Zander, who, at the beginning of the summer, would sometimes turn up on the Nicholses' porch and sit quietly in the swing, hoping (according to Rose, who seemed to know everything) that Abby would come outside and join him. But Abby watched him from the parlor and discovered that she felt as listless then as she did at any other time, and eventually Zander stopped coming by.

And now it was autumn again and she was a freshman at the Barnegat Point high school — a lowly freshman on the bottom rung of the ladder. There was no Rose to walk with, and no Sarah or Orrin to greet her at the gathering spot on the lawn.

"Are you going to spend the entire year mooning around?" asked Ellen when Abby sank down at the kitchen table after school one day, a stack of books at her elbow.

Abby frowned. "What?"

Ellen turned from the stove and faced her. "For pity's sake, honey, Sarah is the one who drowned, not you. You've got your whole life ahead. Stop wasting it."

"I —" said Abby. Tears sprang to her eyes.

"Go ahead and cry. Lord knows you've been through enough. But then you'd better get on with things. I'm speaking plain because no one else seems willing to. They're all still tiptoeing around like you'll break. But I know a thing or two, and you'll break if you don't sit yourself up and get going again. Isn't there something you want to do this year besides schoolwork?"

Abby shook her head.

"There's got to be something. A play or a club? And what about friends? A nice girl like you should have plenty of friends."

"I don't know."

"It isn't easy to find new friends, but you have to make some kind of effort. You're never going to find friends by sitting at your desk or wheeling Adele up and down the street in the carriage."

Abby poked at a cookie that Ellen had set before her. "I saw a sign for the glee club," she ventured.

"Well, that's wonderful. I was in the glee club when I was in school."

Abby had a hard time imagining Ellen as a girl, slim hipped and giggling, standing shoulder to shoulder with her glee club friends. "Really?"

"Yes."

"I saw a sign for the school annual, too," Abby went on. "I'd love to work on the annual."

"There you go. Now, tomorrow, when you get to school, you do whatever it is you have to do to try out for the glee club and work on the annual."

"All right." Abby brightened. Not even the sight of her mother in bed in the middle of the afternoon could dampen her spirits. The next day, feeling resolute, if not exactly cheerful, she found a sign about glee club tryouts and decided to sing "Amazing Grace" as her audition piece. And she signed up to work on the Barnegat Point Central High School 1936–37 Annual.

Now it was the afternoon of September 22nd, four days after the tryouts, and the day the results were to be posted. Abby, a pile of books under her arm, left her last class and hurried through the halls to the principal's office. Two girls were standing by the bulletin board next to the office door, and Abby recognized them as freshmen she'd seen at the tryouts, girls from the village of St. George. She stood on tiptoe and peered at a sheet of paper with the heading WELCOME, NEW GLEE CLUB MEMBERS!

Sixteen names were listed. Abby's was not there. She checked again to make sure and then she stepped back, once again feeling hot tears prick her eyes.

"Don't be upset," said one of the girls. Darcy? Darcy Peters? "Hardly any freshmen ever get into the glee club. We didn't make it either. You can try again next year."

Abby nodded mutely.

She saw the girls glance at each other. After a moment, one of them said, "We're going to Drugs for ice cream. Want to come with us?"

Abby smiled. The drugstore was owned by Mr. Wyatt,

but the sign out front didn't say WYATT'S or even DRUGSTORE, but simply DRUGS, and lots of people, especially the ones who didn't live in Barnegat Point, called the store Drugs.

Abby looked at the girls, at their friendly, curious faces. "Okay," she said, and then added, "I'm Abby. Abby Nichols."

One of them, dark haired and wide-eyed, nodded. "I know. I'm in your English class. I'm Maureen O'Malley."

"Oh!" said Abby. "I'm sorry. I didn't . . ."

"That's okay. I sit way in the back."

The other girl spoke up. "And I'm Darcy Peterson."

"You're both from St. George?" Abby asked.

"Yuh," Maureen replied.

Abby knew instantly that Pop wouldn't approve of Maureen and Darcy. St. George was a tiny coastal community several miles south of Lewisport and, according to Pop, the entire population was lazy. "Not a worker among them," he once said. "I've hired three men from St. George and had to let all of them go inside a week. They never heard of a work ethic down there. Bunch of Catholics anyway."

Abby saw that Maureen's sweater was unraveling at the cuffs and that the fabric of her blouse was thin and shiny. And Darcy's right shoe, she couldn't help noticing, had lost its heel.

"Hey!" she exclaimed suddenly, turning her attention back to Maureen. "I remember you now. You wrote that composition about the seagull and the little boy. That was great. I really liked it." Their teacher had chosen Maureen's from among all the compositions in the class to read aloud one morning.

Abby, Maureen, and Darcy walked slowly through the halls of the high school.

"Have you met the school nurse yet?" asked Darcy as they passed a closed door with a large red cross on it.

Abby shook her head.

"She's gorgeous!" said Maureen.

"She's like a model. She's new here," added Darcy. "I wonder why she became a school nurse in Maine when she could be in pictures. She should be out in Hollywood."

"Her name is Helen March," said Maureen. "That's a good Hollywood name. Boy, I wish I had clothes like hers." She looked down at her own shabby clothes, but said nothing more.

"So do you like it here?" asked Abby finally, feeling supremely self-conscious. What a stupid question. "I mean, here at BPCH?"

"Oh, sure," replied Darcy. "My mother says we're lucky

that this is our high school. She says it's like a fancy school from books, not like our old school in St. George."

"We had to share everything there," Maureen spoke up. "Even desks. But the high school is . . . well, we're like rich girls."

Abby felt herself blush.

"We don't get to go to Drugs very often," said Maureen as they left school and walked across the yard in the sunshine. "I'm saving my money for a coat."

"I'm saving for shoes," said Darcy, and Abby made an effort not to look in the direction of Darcy's missing heel again.

Drugs turned out to be a busy place after school. Abby tried to remember the last time she'd been in the store. Sometime over the summer with Rose, she thought. It had been busy then, too, but not as busy as it was now, filled with chattering students from the high school.

"Let's get a booth," said Maureen, and she slid into the only empty one. Darcy slid in beside her and Abby sat down across from them.

Two thoughts ran through Abby's mind at that moment. *I hope Pop doesn't come in* and *This is fun.*

"What are you going to get?" asked Abby.

"A scoop of vanilla," Darcy replied instantly.

"A scoop of strawberry," said Maureen.

Abby, who had been about to order a sundae with whipped cream, quickly changed her mind and asked the boy who came to take their order for a scoop of chocolate.

The moment the boy had left, Darcy started to giggle. "He's a junior!" she squealed. "He goes to my church. Isn't he cute?"

Maureen turned to Abby. "Don't worry about her. She thinks all boys are cute."

"Well, they are," said Darcy.

Maureen rolled her eyes. "Do you live here in Barnegat Point?" she asked Abby.

Abby nodded. "We used to live in Lewisport, but we moved here a few years ago."

Darcy frowned suddenly. "Your last name is Nichols? Does your father own —"

"Abby!" The door to Drugs had opened and closed, and a tall figure was striding toward Abby's table. Darcy's mouth dropped open.

"Hi, Zander," said Abby.

Zander Burley, resplendent in his Barnegat Point Central High School letterman jacket, stopped at Abby's table, grinned at Darcy and Maureen, and said, "Abby, I didn't know you were going to be here. I have good news for you. We're publishing your poem in *Words*."

"Really?" said Abby, just as Darcy managed to squeak out, "The literary magazine?" and Maureen said, "You submitted a poem to *Words*?"

Zander laughed. "Yes, yes, yes," he said, looking at each of them. "It'll be in the first issue, which comes out in October. See you later."

He loped off, and Abby stared after him. When her ice cream arrived, she smiled at Maureen and Darcy. Okay, so she hadn't made the glee club, but she'd taken Ellen's advice and signed up to work on the annual, one of her poems was actually going to be published — by Zander, no less — and she was sitting in Drugs with two new friends. She pushed an image of Sarah out of her mind, and then an image of Pop, and hoped the subject of her father wouldn't come up again for a while.

"See you tomorrow!" Abby called to Maureen and Darcy as they left Drugs later.

And Darcy replied, "We'll meet you on the lawn in the morning!"

Abby walked slowly toward Haddon Road, arms wrapped around her books, hugging them as tightly as she hugged the thought of new friends and a new school year. She looked down at her shoes, which were also new, and watched her feet for a while, and when she glanced up, she saw Sarah standing at the corner of Haddon. Her arms were crossed and she was watching Abby curiously. Abby almost let out a shriek before she realized that there was nothing at all at the corner except the memory of her very best friend.

Chapter 12

"Maureen! Darcy!" called Abby. She turned the corner from Haddon onto the main street and ran to meet her friends.

"Hi, Abby!" they replied, and linked their arms with hers. They hurried through town toward school, three across, dropping their arms only to avoid running into a large group of men standing outside the bank.

"Town's crowded this morning," Darcy remarked.

"Where are your parents?" asked Abby.

"Mine are already at school," Maureen replied. "They dropped Darcy and me here just so we could walk with you."

"Mine aren't coming," said Darcy, and Abby knew better than to question this.

"I like not having to go to school until ten o'clock," said Maureen. "I wish school started at ten every day."

"Well, summer vacation is here," Abby replied. "You won't have to think about school again for three months."

"Hey, there are Hazel and Jo," said Darcy. "Come on! Let's catch up with them."

"Everyone is all dressed up," Abby said breathlessly as they ran along. "Even the parents."

"I'll bet you win an award today," Maureen said to Abby. "Two, maybe."

"I don't know." Abby blushed.

"Oh, come on. Don't pretend to be modest. You know you're going to win the English award. At least."

Abby grinned. "You think so?"

They reached the lawn in front of the school, caught up with Hazel and Jo, and joined the other kids streaming through the doorway. A teacher hustled them into the auditorium. "Students, please sit in the first four rows," he called. "Parents and other guests, please sit behind the students."

Abby looked at the stage, where an American flag was standing and a row of chairs had been arranged behind a podium. The windows in the auditorium were open and a breeze rustled the curtains, scenting the room with roses and sea air and sun-warmed bricks. She turned and scanned the rows behind her for her parents. She didn't see them. They were probably at home waiting for Sheila, who hadn't arrived by the time Abby had left for school. She was late, which was unlike Sheila.

"Abby!" A hand tapped her knee and she faced front again. Catherine McCann, whose family had moved in across the street from Zander, had slid into the seat in front of her. "Want to go to the pictures tonight?" she asked.

Abby hesitated. The last time she'd been in the movie theatre was almost a month earlier, and she'd seen the Movietone News coverage of the explosion of the Hindenburg. The image of the giant airship suddenly bursting into flame and crashing to the earth had frightened her, and for several nights after that, she'd had trouble sleeping, unable to banish the pictures from her head.

"*Modern Times* is playing. Again," said Catherine.

"Charlie Chaplin?" replied Abby. "All right."

"Attention, please! Attention!" Mr. Sampson, the principal, stood at the podium and tapped the microphone, which squealed.

The bustling auditorium quieted, and Abby turned around once more to look for her parents. She had reminded them that morning to come early or they might not get seats.

"Everyone goes to the award ceremony," she'd said. "And this is *high school*. It's important."

"We'll be there," Mama had replied.

"Where's Sheila?" had been Pop's response. "She should be here already. She's half an hour late."

Abby scanned the faces in the back rows and caught sight of a pair of slightly mismatched gray eyes — one bigger than the other, the smaller one drooping — and a mouth with a thin line of saliva leaking from the corner.

Fred.

He was sitting in Mama's lap. Pop was next to them, his mouth set in a grim line, leaning slightly away so that people might think he had come by himself, that Fred and Mama belonged to some other student.

Abby whirled around, faced front, then looked over her shoulder again. Where was Sheila? If Fred was here, then Sheila must not have shown up. Adele could be left behind with Ellen, but Fred couldn't. Pop was sure to be furious. Furious with Sheila and furious at having to appear in public with Fred.

Abby turned her attention back to Mr. Sampson, who tapped the microphone again, letting out an even louder, more shrill squeal than before. The squeal was matched by a shriek from the back of the room.

"Iiiiiiiiiiiieeeee*eeeee*!"

The shriek increased in intensity, and Abby didn't need to turn around to know that it was Fred, who had absolutely no tolerance for loud noises, except his own. She slumped in her seat and was relieved when the shrieking stopped abruptly.

"Was that Fred?" whispered Maureen, in alarm.

"Yes. I don't know what he's doing here."

"Lots of little kids are here," Darcy pointed out.

Abby nodded. She and Maureen and Darcy had been friends for nine months, but she had never invited them to her house. Not once. Most days they wouldn't have been able to go anyway. They had chores at home, younger brothers and sisters to care for, which was a relief to Abby. She didn't dare introduce them to Pop, and she certainly didn't want them to see her big house. She knew they'd heard about it. She couldn't keep her life a complete secret. But they didn't need to meet the maid, the baby nurse, the gardener — not when they had to play all those roles themselves at their own homes.

They'd met Fred, though, on two occasions when their families had come to Barnegat Point on a weekend, and they'd run into Abby taking Fred for a walk around town. To Abby's relief, they hadn't seemed bothered by Fred, not even when she had explained that he couldn't walk or talk yet, and although they could see his uneven features, plain as day.

Abby sat up again and tried to pay attention. Fred had stopped squawking, the microphone had stopped squawking, and Mr. Sampson was saying, "We'll start with the freshman awards, then move to the sophomore awards, the junior awards, and finally, the overall awards."

Abby looked up and down the four rows of students. There were 126 of them, she knew. The seniors, who had graduated two nights before, were not present. Their high school careers were over. Most of them would start jobs that summer and most of the boys would continue working those jobs for a long, long time. The girls would soon get married and have babies. Only five of the seniors were going to college in the fall, four of them boys. The lone girl, Marjorie Mullion, would be attending Smith College in Northampton, Massachusetts. Abby wondered what it would feel like to receive your high school diploma and know that in a few short months you'd be leaving your family and the town you'd grown up in, and moving to a school where every single face would belong to a stranger.

What would Abby be doing in three years? Maureen wanted to get a job working for the telephone company, and Darcy planned to get married as soon as she graduated and become a wife and a mother, although there was no boy in her life yet. Abby couldn't see herself working for the telephone company (even if Pop would allow it, which he wouldn't), and she couldn't see herself raising a family either. Not right away. College? That was a scary proposi —

"Abby! *Abby!*" Maureen was saying, and Darcy nudged her in the ribs. "Go up on the stage! He just called your name for the history award."

Abby leaped to her feet. She realized that everyone was applauding. For her.

"Congratulations," said Mr. Sampson as Abby approached him. He handed her a piece of paper rolled into a tube and tied with a pale blue ribbon.

"Thank you," said Abby, and shook his hand. She started to walk off the stage, but Mr. Sampson caught her arm. "Stay right where you are."

Abby looked out at the audience in alarm. She tried to catch her mother's eye, but she and Pop were struggling with Fred, who looked on the verge of a tantrum.

"The next award," said Mr. Sampson, "our Freshman High Achievement Award, goes to . . . Abigail Nichols."

Abby heard clapping and cheers and, from one seat by the windows, a loud whistle. When she had collected the second award and returned to her seat, Maureen hugged her and said, "I told you so," and Darcy made her unroll the certificates so they could read them. Abby's heart was pounding and she felt flushed, but she managed to sit calmly through the sophomore and junior awards, grateful to hear no more angry sounds from Fred. When Mr. Sampson presented the Junior English Award, Abby said, "Zander won that last year." And then to her embarrassment, she started to giggle, which prompted Darcy to say, "He's not your husband . . . yet."

"And now," Mr. Sampson went on, "it's time for the overall awards."

Abby heard a wail from the back of the room then, followed by a crash. She winced and turned around. Pop was on his feet, the seat of his chair having whacked back into place, and Mama was getting to her feet more delicately, handing Fred to Pop as she did so. Fred began to kick and flail and Abby heard his familiar *iiiiiieeeeeee* again.

"Excuse us, pardon, pardon us," said Pop, grim faced, as he edged along the row to the aisle, holding Fred in front of him not as if he were a four-year-old boy, but as if he were a naughty cat that he intended to put out on the porch. "Excuse us."

Abby faced front again and tried to ignore the commotion. Mr. Sampson flashed her a smile, raised his voice slightly, and continued the ceremony, as if he didn't hear a thing. "The Overall Mathematics Award," he said, "goes to Michael O'Malley."

Abby opened her mouth and gaped at Maureen, who was gaping back at her. "Your brother!" exclaimed Abby, and Maureen jumped to her feet and began clapping.

The cheering hadn't quite ended when Mr. Sampson said, "And the Overall English Award goes to Abigail Nichols."

Abby rose uncertainly while Maureen and Darcy tugged at her arms, laughing, and she walked once more to the stage.

"Congratulations," said Mr. Sampson again. "Well done."

Abby felt her eyes drawn to the empty seats at the back of the room, but then she noticed movement in the doorway and saw Mama waving to her through the small window. Abby flashed her a smile and returned to her seat.

When the program ended a few minutes later, she turned to Darcy and Maureen and said, "Come on. They're going to hand out our annuals now. I want you to be the first to sign mine."

She turned around and ran directly into Zander. Abby clapped her hand to her mouth, then dropped it to her side and exclaimed, "What are you doing here?"

Zander grinned. "I figured you'd win a bunch of awards. I didn't want to miss out. Congratulations."

Abby glanced helplessly at Maureen and Darcy. Maureen touched her shoulder. "Darcy and I will wait for you outside," she whispered, and disappeared down the aisle, with Darcy in her wake.

"Were you here for the whole program?" Abby asked Zander.

"The whole thing. And before you ask, yes, I heard Fred." Abby dropped her eyes.

"Actually, I agree with Fred," Zander went on. "I felt like screaming, too. I thought Mr. Sampson would never stop talking. Now come on. Gather up your awards, if you can carry them all. I'll walk outside with you."

Chapter 13

Friday, October 29th, 1937

"But everyone's going!" said Rose, and Abby heard a whine creep into her sister's voice. "Everyone."

Rose was thirteen and, in Abby's opinion, too old to whine. It certainly wasn't helping their case.

"I've already said no," Pop replied. "Don't ask me about this again."

"But my costume is half finished. I'll bet no one else is going to be Tiger Lily!"

"I told you no last night when your costume was only a third finished. Why is it half finished now when I already told you that you can't go to the party?"

Rose shrugged. "This is so unfair!"

"Rose," said Pop, "come here."

Rose hesitated. She was standing in the doorway to the dining room, where Pop was seated at the table with Mama, while Ellen served them breakfast. "Never mind," she said hastily. "Sorry." She turned away. "Sorry," she said again.

Abby followed her sister up the stairs to her room. "Don't antagonize him like that. Why do you do it?"

"I want to go to the Halloween party! There's never been a Halloween party here before, and I don't want to miss it. Just think of all the costumes."

"I queen," announced a voice from behind them, and Abby turned to see Adele, still in her nightdress, standing sleepily in the hallway. "I queen," she said again.

Abby bent to pick up her sister. "Sorry, sissy," she said. "We can't go to the party after all."

"But I queen!"

Abby let out a sigh. She had heard tales of kids dressing in costume and going door-to-door in their neighborhoods on Halloween night, collecting candy. But trick-or-treating hadn't reached Barnegat Point yet. Halloween was barely celebrated. This year, however, a Halloween party for all ages was to be held at the high school. The guests were going to attend in costume, and there would be games and prizes and bobbing for apples. Abby, Maureen, and Darcy, sophomores now, had planned to dress as the Three Musketeers. Now Athos and Porthos would have to go without Aramis.

"Buy *why* won't Pop let us go?" wailed Rose, throwing herself dramatically on her bed. "Halloween is on Sunday but the party is on Saturday. It isn't as if we're asking to go to a party on the Lord's day."

"He just doesn't approve," Abby replied, setting Adele on the floor. "It's Halloween — witches and spirits and black magic. That sort of thing. So you'd better be quiet about this unless you want to get into trouble. Pop has said no a hundred times already."

"I don't care. I'm going to sneak out," said Rose, sitting up suddenly. "I'm going to finish my costume after school today and sneak out tomorrow night. Pop won't know."

Abby glanced at Adele.

"Oh, she won't say anything," said Rose.

"She might. Anyway, how are you going to sneak out? Go out your window and jump down from the second story? You'll kill yourself."

Rose turned away. "I'll think of something."

After school Abby met Rose at the corner of Haddon and they walked the rest of the way home together.

"So," said Rose, "did you tell Darcy and Maureen that you aren't going to the party?"

"Yes." Abby kicked at a stone.

"Are they mad?"

"Sort of."

"So come with me tomorrow. You don't have to stay home from the party, Miss Goody Two-Shoes."

Abby shook her head. Then she stopped in her tracks. "What's Pop's car doing in the drive?" she asked. "Why is he home now? It's only three-thirty."

Rose turned pale. "You don't think Adele told him about my plan, do you?"

"I don't know. Probably not. And maybe nothing is wrong. But still." Abby began to run. When she reached the porch, she bounded up the steps and flung the front door open.

"I'll bet it's just something silly," said Rose hopefully from behind her.

But Abby found Mama sitting on an armchair in the parlor, crying, Pop standing next to her, looking grim. From the kitchen Abby could hear tight, anxious voices, and in a flash she was at the edge of the pond on that snowy December day again, watching Sarah fall unstoppably through the ice.

"What's wrong?" Abby whispered. She took off her coat and let it slide to the floor. "Where's Adele? Where's Fred? What's the matter?"

"Girls, come here," said Mama. She pulled a hankie from her pocket and dabbed at her eyes. "Your father has something to tell you." She glared at Pop, then reached for Abby's hand. "Sit, sit."

Abby glanced at Rose and sat awkwardly on the edge of a horsehair sofa, pulling Rose down next to her. "What is it, Pop?"

Pop cleared his throat. "I took Fred to a school today."

"You took Fred to a school?" Rose repeated. "What school?"

"A very nice school where he can live with other children like himself."

"Live?" Abby gasped, and looked again at her mother's eyes, swollen and puffy. Now she knew the reason for her tears. *"Live?"*

"There's a farm on the property where the children grow vegetables," Pop continued, "and there are yards to play in, and beautiful dormitories. The teachers have been specially trained to work with the feebleminded. They'll know just how to deal with Fred."

Abby jumped up from the sofa and cried, "But nobody knows how to take care of Fred like Sheila and I do!"

"It's a better place for him," said Pop.

"Better than his own home? Pop, he's never spent a single night away from us. How could you just give him away?" Abby turned to her mother. "How could you let him?"

Mama bowed her head. "I didn't know he . . . I didn't know what was going to happen."

"You did this in *secret?*" exclaimed Abby. She got to her feet, but Rose shoved her back onto the couch and stepped toward Pop.

"Tell us about the classrooms at this school," said Rose. "Tell us what kind of *learning* Fred is going to get."

Abby yanked Rose's hand, but to her surprise Pop regarded his daughters evenly. "He'll learn what he can learn. And he'll be with other people like himself."

"How old are these other people?" asked Rose.

"Fred's age all the way up to adult."

"I'll bet there aren't many other five-year-olds who get sent to institutions," muttered Abby.

"This is a school with —" Pop started to say.

"You mean an *institution,*" Rose interrupted him.

"This is a *school* with a dining hall and playgrounds. And nurses and doctors. They'll work with Fred. So will the teachers. He'll learn to walk and talk, maybe even read."

"Why didn't you tell us about this wonderful school before now?" asked Abby.

Pop frowned at her, but before he could say anything, Rose asked, "Where is the school?"

"In Powell."

Powell. Sixty miles away.

Mama stood and brushed her hands briskly down her

front, as if she were wearing an apron, which she wasn't. "I insist that we bring Fred back immediately," she said, addressing the fireplace.

"No," said Pop.

"What's the name of this school? I'll go there myself and bring him home."

"How? You don't even know how to drive."

Mama spun around and faced Pop. "Mike will take me there. Or I'll take a train. I'll find the school even if you won't tell me its name."

"Nell," said Pop, "I simply don't understand why you would want to deprive Fred of an opportunity like this. Weren't you listening to me? This is a beautiful place — hills and barns and lots of children for Fred to play with. You want that for him, don't you?"

"Fred's never been away from home. He doesn't know anyone but us. He must be terrified." Mama put her hand to her throat.

"How could you do this without even letting us say good-bye to him?" asked Rose.

"It was better this way," Pop replied. "Surely you can see that. I didn't want to upset him."

"Abby," said Rose, "do something!"

Abby frowned. "How many other kids there are Fred's age?" she asked.

"Plenty. Enough for a whole dormitory of five-year-olds."

"Do you really think Fred will learn to walk now?" Abby had spent an entire summer trying to teach him herself.

"Definitely."

Rose gaped at Abby. "You're taking Pop's side? He took away your own baby brother and abandoned him in a strange place —"

"Rose," said Pop, in a voice barely above a whisper. "Get upstairs right now."

"Stay where you are, Rose," said Mama, just as quietly. "Luther, if we aren't going to bring Fred home for good, then I insist that we visit him immediately."

Pop shook his head. "We aren't allowed to visit for six months. That's how long it takes the . . . students to settle in."

Mama sank back into her chair. Pop glanced at Rose, who ran upstairs. Then he knelt beside Mama.

"Look, Nell," he said, and placed his hand on her arm.

Mama jerked away. "Don't touch me. Do not ever touch me."

Abby tiptoed into the kitchen. She found Ellen and Sheila

seated at the table. Sheila had pulled her apron to her face and was sobbing into it.

"Fred is just like a baby. A *baby*," cried Sheila. "You don't give away a little baby." Ellen patted her arm.

"Where's Adele?" asked Abby, and Sheila jumped.

"Sorry. I didn't mean to startle you. But where is Adele?"

"Asleep," Sheila replied, wiping her eyes. "She kept asking where Fred is and your father told her the fairies took him. She wore herself out crying."

Abby returned to the parlor. She found Pop standing next to the fireplace, staring out the window at the darkening street. "Where's Mama?" she asked.

Pop shrugged. "Probably in her room."

"I can't believe this," Abby said after a moment. "How could you do this behind our backs? You didn't even let Mama say good-bye to Fred. Not even *Mama*. He's her baby."

Pop turned. "I did what I thought was right."

"You did what you thought was easiest."

Pop whirled around and Abby fled up the stairs. She paused for a moment, and when she didn't hear Pop's footsteps behind her, she knocked on the door to Mama's room.

"Mama?" No answer. She opened the door anyway. Mama was seated in a chair, gazing out her window. A junco was perched on the bare branch of a tree.

"Please go away, Abby."

"Are you all right?"

"I asked you to go away."

Abby passed the closed door to Adele's room — the room that, until this morning, she had shared with Fred — and the closed door to Rose's room, shut her own door, and sat on her bed. Maybe Fred would learn things at the school that she hadn't been able to teach him. Maybe. But she would never, ever have done what Pop had done. He had given away a five-year-old, and he had broken Mama's fragile heart.

Chapter 14

The new clothing store opened in Barnegat Point shortly after elderly Mr. Haworth closed his shop in January. Miss Amelia Compton, who had helped the ladies and young girls of Barnegat Point select their clothing at Haworth's for nearly twenty years, refused the offer to work for Miss Irene Maynard, who had bought Haworth's and immediately changed the name to Maynard's. Miss Amelia said she had never worked for a woman and that she didn't intend to start now. She added that it wasn't natural for a woman to own her own business, and that, furthermore, Irene Maynard wasn't actually *Miss* Maynard, but a divorcée — unlike Miss Amelia, who came by her spinsterhood honestly. Even worse, Irene Maynard used rouge, wore suggestive dresses and inappropriate hats, and occasionally smoked a pipe.

Miss Amelia was extremely suspicious of Miss Irene Maynard, but the rest of Barnegat Point was fascinated by her. Everyone stopped by Maynard's to take a look at the possible divorcée, if not to actually buy clothes from her.

Maynard's had been open for two months of dreary business when, on one of the first warm days of spring, Abby walked home from school alone, dawdling, missing Darcy and Maureen, who had both stayed home with colds, and daydreaming about Richard Lord, the new boy in her class. She passed the drugstore, noticing that Richard was there with two boys from Lewisport, passed the movie theatre, and then found herself looking in the window of Maynard's. She studied the pastel-colored dresses on display, remembering the years when Mama had made new Easter dresses for her and Rose, and wondering whether she should go inside to try something on. She had no money for a dress, but surely Pop would want her to look nice in church on Sunday. He would give her the money for a new dress if she asked.

The door to Maynard's was flung open suddenly and Miss Maynard herself leaned out into the mild air. "Would you like to come inside and look around?" she asked Abby.

"Oh, n —" Abby was about to say that she wouldn't be able to buy anything just then, but instead found herself entering the little shop curiously.

Miss Maynard held out her hand to Abby. "I'm Irene Maynard," she said. The hand she offered was warm, and

Abby held it for just an instant as she took in the sight of Barnegat Point's newcomer. Miss Maynard was young, probably not ten years older than Abby, and she was wearing a polka-dotted dress cut low enough to fascinate every one of Abby's classmates, male and female — and to outrage Pop. Her hair was piled high on her head, with wispy tendrils winding around her face. Abby studied its color long enough to decide that it was the result of an encounter with a bottle of bleach.

Abby almost replied, "I know," since everyone in town knew who Irene Maynard was, but she remembered her manners in time and said, "I'm Abby Nichols." Then she added, "We used to shop here when this was Haworth's."

"I'm pleased to meet you. Would you like to try on one of the dresses? The blue one, maybe? That's a good color for you."

"I — Actually, I don't have any money. I mean, I'd have to ask my father if I could buy the dress, and . . ."

Miss Maynard looked Abby over from top to bottom, taking in her clothing (nicer, Abby knew, than the clothing of many of her classmates) and her schoolbooks. "Would you like to work here this summer?" she asked suddenly.

"What?" said Abby.

"Would you like a part-time job? I could use some help here. I'm running the store myself, which is fine while things are quiet, but in the summer I'm sure I'll need another pair of hands."

"But I've never worked in a store," Abby replied. "I've never had a job at all. I mean, except for working on the school annual, and that isn't really a job."

"Are you a good student?"

"Yes."

"Are you organized?"

"Yes, I think so."

"Do you think you could learn the job? Are you a quick study?"

"Yes."

Miss Maynard smiled at Abby. "How old are you?"

"I'll be sixteen next month."

"Perfect. You have a job."

"I'd better ask my father for permission first."

"All right. Talk to him tonight and come see me again tomorrow."

Abby walked the rest of the way home, dreaming of being a working girl, even if it was just for the summer, and of earning her own money and getting a taste of independence. She'd be able to buy clothes without asking Pop for money, and she could spend all day in town working a cash register and never, ever telling little kids not to touch anything.

Abby approached her house slowly. When she reached the lawn, she glanced automatically at the window on the second floor, the one at the corner, facing the street. The shade was drawn. Abby sighed. She let herself inside, called hello to Ellen and Sheila, then climbed the stairs and knocked on her mother's door.

"Mama?" she said softly.

When there was no answer, Abby cracked the door open and peeked into the darkened room. Mama was in bed asleep, still wearing her nightdress, breathing deeply and evenly. Abby closed the door again and tiptoed downstairs.

She found Sheila and Adele in the kitchen, making cookies while Ellen started dinner.

"Did Mama get up today?" Abby asked.

"She has been asleep the whole long day," Adele announced. "The whole long day."

Abby looked at Ellen, who nodded but said nothing.

"Can I go outside now?" asked Adele.

"As soon as I clean up this mess," replied Sheila.

"I'll take her out," said Abby. "It's so nice today. Come on, Adele."

Abby and Adele walked hand in hand to the front porch and were sitting on the swing when Rose returned from school and ran into the house, announcing that she was starving.

"Let's play a game," said Adele.

"All right. What do you want to play?"

Adele frowned. "Find Fred," she said eventually.

Abby looked sharply at her sister. "How do you play Find Fred?"

"You get in the car and you drive around and around with Mike, and if you see any fairies, you ask them where they took Fred."

Abby pulled Adele into her lap. "You do know where Fred is, don't you?" Adele shook her head. "He's at school," Abby reminded her.

"You and Rose go to school and you come home every single day."

"But Pop took Fred to a special kind of school."

"Is he going to take me to a special kind of school?"

"No. You can go to a regular school like Rose and I do."

"But why did Pop take —"

"Abby! Hello!"

"Hi, Wyman," said Abby, startled, getting to her feet.

"Hi, Wyman," echoed Adele, even though she had never met the boy who was striding across the Nicholses' lawn.

"Hi, Wyman." Rose's voice floated out through the parlor window behind Abby.

Abby glanced over her shoulder, said, "Shh," to the window, and then turned her attention to Wyman Todd who, according to Darcy, was the dreamiest boy in the tenth grade.

"Look what I have," said Wyman. He climbed the porch steps, waving a magazine in front of him.

"Oh, is that *In Our Voices*?" Abby leaped up from the swing.

Wyman grinned at her. "Yes, and your story is in here."

"How did you get an early copy? Oh, never mind. Could I see it, please?"

Wyman sat on the swing and pulled Abby down after him. "That's why I brought it over. Turn to page twenty-four."

Abby opened the magazine and leafed through it, ignoring the whispered voice behind her that said, "Woo-hoo, he's sweet on you!"

"It's so exciting to see it in print," said Abby. "My very own story."

"You've seen your poems in print before. Zander put plenty of your poems in *Words*."

Abby glanced automatically across the yard at the Burleys' house, and her eyes drifted to the window that had been

Zander's. Well, it was still Zander's, she supposed, but he had been away at college — his first year at Harvard, an impressive fact that Pop never tired of pointing out — and his absence was almost as arresting as any unexpected glimpse of him through his bedroom window had been.

"Yes, but this is different," said Abby, turning her attention back to Wyman. "It's an actual story. I feel like an author. Thank you *so* much for bringing this by." She took Wyman by the hand, while Adele looked on in fascination and Wyman blushed a brilliant shade of pink.

"You're welcome," he mumbled.

"I wrote a story," said Adele, climbing into Wyman's lap.

"Did you?"

"Yes. It's about a fairy. A boy fairy like Peter Pan. His name was Hankie and he lived in a flower and one day he left the flower and got lost and the rest of the fairies found him and took him home and the mother fairy was glad to see Hankie and kissed him and never let him get lost again." Adele paused. "The end."

"That's a very nice story," said Wyman. Then he set Adele on her feet and stood up. "Well, I have to go." He started to reach for *In Our Voices*, glanced at the street where Pop's car was turning into the drive, and said, "You can keep it. I'll get another," before running across the lawn.

161

In the drive, Pop slammed the door of his newest car, and glared after Wyman. Then he strode to the porch and said, "Abigail, what have I told you about entertaining young men?"

Pop had not actually told Abby anything about entertaining young men, since no young men except Zander had ever visited her.

"It wasn't as though we were alone. Ellen and Sheila are right inside," said Abby. "Adele was with me, and Rose has been spying on us."

"I have not!" cried Rose, appearing in the window.

Pop grunted and sat down in a chair. "Where's your mother?" he asked.

"Upstairs. Pop, could I ask you something?"

"Sure."

"You know the new store? The one that used to be Haworth's?"

"Yuh."

"Well, the lady who owns it — Miss Maynard — asked me if I'd like to work there this summer. She said she could use help when things get busy."

"What do you need a job for?"

"To earn money."

"Don't I give you plenty of money?"

"Yes. But I'd like to earn my own, and not have to ask you every time I want to buy something."

"Abby, I can't have people thinking I don't earn enough money to support this family. And that's exactly what they'll think if they see you behind the counter in that store."

"How about if she worked in a different store?" called Rose. "What would people think then?"

"Rose!" Abby called out.

There was a clatter and then the sound of Rose's feet disappearing upstairs.

"Could you think it over, Pop, please? I told Miss Maynard I'd give her an answer tomorrow."

"The answer is no."

"You're not even going to think about it?"

"I don't have to. You're not going to work. Especially not for that woman."

"What's wrong with Miss Maynard?"

Pop floundered for a moment. "She's pushy," he said finally. "And divorced."

"Zander's going to work this summer before he goes back to Harvard."

"Zander is a boy. He has to learn how to support himself."

"But won't people think Mr. Burley can't support his own family?"

"Not one more smart word out of you, young lady," said Pop. "No job. The subject is closed."

Just like that, the subject was snapped shut, which, Abby realized, was how her father handled anything unpleasant. He snapped the lid shut on Fred, on her mother, on Abby's cynical questions, and he refused to open it again.

Chapter 15

"It's different without Mama, isn't it?" said Rose, her gaze fixed at a point on the blazing horizon of the Atlantic Ocean. "Two weeks here at the cottage, but without Mama. And without Fred."

Abby, Rose, and Adele were used to visiting the house in Lewisport without Pop, and recently without Fred, but always, always Mama had been there.

"In a way," replied Abby, "it's as if she's here with us. It's strange, but I can almost smell her."

Rose turned to look at her sister. "I stole her rosewater before we left," she whispered.

"Rose! The whole bottle?"

"It isn't as though she's going to miss it. She hasn't gotten out of bed in weeks."

This was why Abby, Rose, and Adele were on vacation at the cottage with Uncle Marshall and Aunt Betty but no Mama. Mama was feeble. She was frail. Night after night,

Abby sat with her in her room in the house on Haddon Road, stroking her hands, telling her about the events of the day, and studying her face. She could see spidery blue veins crawling along beneath Mama's ghostly skin.

Mama had stopped asking about Fred. Sometimes she asked if the rosebushes were all right, but she didn't ask about Fred.

When the subject of two weeks at the cottage had come up, Pop had said, "Maybe Betty and Marshall will take you girls." The trip was out of the question for Mama. And Pop would stay in Barnegat Point to work.

"Abby!" Aunt Betty called now. "Rose!"

Abby turned to look across the street at Mama's sister, who was leaning out the front door of the house.

"Make sure you keep an eye on Adele. The waves are rough today."

"We're watching!" Rose shouted back. She adjusted herself on the wooden beach chair while Abby fixed her attention on Adele, who was busy digging a hole in the sand.

"It's a fairy hole," Adele had informed her earlier.

"What's a fairy hole?" Abby had asked.

Adele had frowned and pointed at the hole. *"That,"* she had replied, and continued digging.

"This is strange," Abby said after a long silence.

"What is?"

"All the people who used to be here with us — well, most of the people — are gone now. No Fred, no Sarah, no Orrin, no Mama, not even any of our cousins."

"Well, it isn't as if they're dead," said Rose, and caught herself. "I mean, Sarah is, but, you know, Orrin's just away, and so is Fred. Mama's at home, and Blaine and everyone are . . . old. Hey, can you believe Erma's going to have a baby? What will that make us? Aunts?"

Abby shook her head. "Some kind of cousins, I think. Cousins once removed? Anyway, not aunts."

"I want to be an aunt."

"Don't look at me," said Abby. "I have to get married and have a baby before you can be an aunt."

"You should marry Orrin. I know you still write to each other."

Abby made a face. Orrin wrote back only one letter for every five of hers.

"What time is it?" asked Rose lazily.

"I don't know. Almost lunchtime, maybe. We should take Adele back to the house. She's going to need a bath."

"Hey!" exclaimed Rose. "Who's that?"

Abby turned away from Adele and shaded her eyes as a car, a shiny new black car, barreled along Blue Harbor Lane and came to a fast stop in front of the cottage, sending out a spray of sand and gravel. The car door was flung open.

"It's Mr. Burley!" said Abby. "What's he doing here?" She watched as Zander's father ran to the cottage and pounded on the door. "Come on, we'd better see what's happening."

Abby took Adele by the hand and ran her across the street. Rose reached the cottage ahead of them. They burst inside in time to hear Mr. Burley say to Aunt Betty and Uncle Marshall, "I'm sorry to be the bearer of bad news, but Luther didn't think you'd want to hear this over the telephone."

"Where's Pop?" Rose demanded. "Why didn't *he* come to tell us the news?"

Mr. Burley turned to look at Abby, Rose, and Adele, and his face softened. "Girls," he said. "Why don't you sit down?" He glanced at the sofa in the little front room.

"Maybe we don't want to sit down!" said Rose, her voice rising. But a shaken-looking Aunt Betty steered her toward the sofa and placed her hands on her shoulders. "Sit, honey."

Rose sat. Abby sat next to her.

"I think maybe I'll take Adele back to the beach," said Uncle Marshall, looking from his wife to Mr. Burley.

Mr. Burley nodded. "That might be a good idea."

Aunt Betty dropped to the couch and squeezed herself between Abby and Rose. She took their hands. "It's Nell, isn't it," she said flatly.

Mr. Burley bowed his head. He was holding his hat in his hands, turning it back and forth as if it were a steering wheel. "Yes. I'm sorry. I'm so sorry. She passed away this morning. Just a little while ago."

Abby felt that some sort of outburst was expected, but she couldn't muster one, not right now.

"How did she die?" Rose whispered.

Mr. Burley looked uncomfortable. "She just . . . passed away. In her sleep. She was . . . she was very weak." He glanced at Aunt Betty.

Abby suddenly realized that Aunt Betty had lost her sister. She let go of her aunt's hand and put her arms around her instead, and Betty sobbed into her neck.

"What are we supposed to do now?" asked Rose in a hushed voice.

"Let me think. Just let me think," said Aunt Betty. She got to her feet. "There will have to be a funeral, of course. And we'll have to get your house ready for visitors."

"Aunt Betty?" said Abby. "What do we tell Adele?"

Aunt Betty was wearing a strand of glass beads around her neck — pale, milky blue, the color of the sky before a storm sets up — and she twisted the beads around her forefinger, twisting and twisting until Abby thought the string would break. Finally she said, "Let's just get you girls home first."

"Where's Mama?" asked Rose.

A pause. "At the hospital," Mr. Burley replied. "Your father is with her."

"Will we see her again?" asked Abby.

"I don't know."

Abby glared at him, hating him for being Pop's stand-in even though she knew Pop was where he ought to be. "Excuse me," she said. She left the front room and walked primly through the cottage and out the back door to the spot where the rosebushes had once grown. She sat down carefully in the sandy soil and thought about Mama and the dead babies, and about the living ones who hadn't seemed to matter as much to her as the dead ones.

Everything has changed, thought Abby. *Just like that, we're a different family now.* She found that she needed to steady herself. She thrust one hand forward and rested it in the soil as she felt — she was sure of this — the earth slip a little.

The ride back to Barnegat Point seemed endless. Aunt Betty, Uncle Marshall, Abby, Rose, and Adele followed Mr. Burley back to Haddon Road in silence.

"Why is nobody talking?" asked Adele.

Rose glanced at Abby.

"We have a little emergency," said Abby, after a moment. "Do you know what an emergency is?"

"Something bad?"

"Well, something we have to take care of right away. Pop wants us back home."

"Why?"

Now Abby glanced at Betty, but her aunt was pressing a hankie to her lips, her chin quivering.

"Because Mama's . . . sick."

"Does she have the throwing-up sickness like I did?"

"No. She —"

"Adele, quit talking for a minute and be quiet," said Rose. "Just be quiet."

"That is not nice," said Adele fiercely, glaring at her sister. "The fairies are going to get you."

When Mr. Burley turned onto Haddon, he had to park in his own driveway instead of in the Nicholses'.

"Whose cars are those?" asked Abby. "Who's at our house?" There were two cars in their drive and several more in the street.

"Pop's back," said Rose. "And there's Mrs. Evans."

Ellen was opening the front door to nosy Mrs. Evans, who was holding a dish covered in a blue-checked cloth.

Abby, Rose, and Adele hurried up the steps after Mrs. Evans and were greeted by Sheila, who had clearly been crying.

"Thank you, Mr. Burley," she said over Abby's shoulder. Then she turned to the girls. "Upstairs with all of you."

"But why are all these people here?" asked Rose.

"News spreads quickly," Sheila replied with distaste, and she shooed the girls up the staircase.

"I want to see Mama," said Adele, "but not her throw-up."

"What?" said Sheila.

"Never mind," said Abby. "Where's Pop?"

"Talking to the cor — Downstairs, I think. You can see him in a little while."

"I don't want to," said Rose, and burst into tears.

Abby put her arms around her. Then she looked at Sheila. "Adele doesn't know yet," she said. "I'll tell her."

"Tell me what?" asked Adele.

"Let's go into your room." Abby led Adele along the hallway as, behind her, Rose slipped into her bedroom and shut the door softly. Sheila disappeared down the stairs.

"Where's Mama?" said Adele. "I thought we were going to see her."

"That's what I need to talk to you about. Here." Abby handed Adele one of her many dolls, a small pink one with painted brown hair, wearing a pleated skirt and party shoes (and nothing else). "Which doll is this?"

"That's Eddie."

"Okay. You hold tight to Eddie and listen to me very carefully." Abby paused. She knew that if Mama were here, she would have told Adele the truth, so after a moment she said, "Adele, do you know what it means when a person dies?"

"Yes."

"What?"

"I don't know."

"Well, it means that the person isn't alive anymore, which means that the person can't come back."

"Okay."

"And Mama died this morning. She had been very sick, and finally her body just couldn't stay alive any longer. So she's gone. She isn't coming back."

Adele stared at her sister. "I don't believe you." She jumped off the bed. "You're wrong. I'll show you."

Abby followed her sister into Mama's room and stood next to her as they both looked at the empty bed.

"Mama?" called Adele. She leaned back into the hall. "Mama?"

Abby took her sister's hand. "She really isn't here, Adele. She's gone."

Adele yanked her hand away. "You tell lies," she said fiercely. "The fairies took her. They took Fred and now they have Mama."

"No." Abby shook her head. "Mama was sick. Remember? She stayed in bed all the time. She was very sick and this morning she died."

"Well, she's still with the fairies."

Abby heard footsteps on the stairs and turned around. She watched Pop's head rise and rise until all six feet of him stood at the other end of the hall. Adele thrust her hand back in Abby's.

"Does she know?" Pop asked Abby, and when she said yes, he let out his breath. "Good. Where's Rose?"

"In her room."

Pop nodded. Then he turned and went back down the stairs.

At the end of the day, after the neighbors had gone home, and Adele and even Rose were finally asleep, and Pop was sitting in the parlor with Aunt Betty and Uncle Marshall, Abby stood in Mama's doorway and studied her room. Sheila had made the bed. Abby couldn't remember the last time she'd seen it clean and unwrinkled, each pillow in place. Two bureau drawers had been left open after Aunt Betty and Ellen had gone through them, looking for Mama's final outfit. The closet door was open, too. Abby stepped into the room and closed the drawers. Then she walked into the closet and stood very still. After a long time she reached for Mama's dressing gown and pulled the sleeve to her nose. She sniffed. Rosewater. She closed the door quietly and went down the hall to her room.

Chapter 16

Abby sat at her dressing table and leaned toward the mirror to examine her lipstick. When she pulled back, she saw Adele standing behind her and she jumped.

"Did I scare you?" asked Adele.

"Well, yes. You shouldn't sneak up on people."

"I didn't sneak up. What are you doing?"

"Getting ready for the dance."

Adele nodded wisely. "With Wyman. You're going with Wyman. He's your beau."

"He's not my —" Abby paused. It was better not to contradict her little sister. "Yes, I'm going with Wyman."

"Well, it's almost my birthday," said Adele, as if this were somehow connected to the subject of Wyman and the dance. "Three more days. Then I will be four years old."

"That's right," Abby agreed. She leaned into the mirror again and held a pair of pearls up to her ears.

"Why is the Valentine's Day dance tonight? Why isn't it on Valentine's Day?"

"Because Valentine's Day is on Tuesday, a school day. It's more fun to go to a dance on Saturday night."

Abby set the pearls down and picked up the single red rose that the florist had delivered that afternoon. Zander wanted her to wear it in her hair, but how? She stuck it behind her ear and it promptly fell onto the dressing table. She wished Mama were there to help her with it, and with about a million other things — her jewelry, for example, and her perfume (Abby had an idea that she had put on way too much) — and to answer some questions about boys that had arisen twelve days earlier when, it seemed, every boy in her life had come calling in one fashion or another.

That day, a Monday, had started off in a mundane manner, but slid out of kilter in the afternoon when Abby realized that she'd misplaced her history notebook. It held her essay entitled "The Influence of History on Seventeenth-Century Music." Abby had nearly panicked before she'd recalled standing up from her desk at the end of her previous class, turning to laugh at Rose, who'd been making faces at her from the hallway, and rushing out of the room, leaving her notebook on her desk.

Abby had raised her hand. "Um, Mr. Fleming? I think I left my notebook behind in English class. Could I please go get it? My essay is in it." She'd ignored wheezy Elvin Burrows, who'd been snickering because Abby had said "behind" and was now pointing to his own.

Mr. Fleming, looking vaguely annoyed, had waved Abby to the door and indicated that Elvin should move to the front row, where he could keep an eye on him.

Abby had hurried into the hallway. She liked walking through the halls of Barnegat Point Central High when classes were in session and the school was a calmer place. She passed her algebra classroom and the library and the freshman science room, where Rose was struggling through her basic biology course. Then she turned a corner, retraced her steps to her English class, knocked on the door, and retrieved her notebook. She'd taken a different route back to Mr. Fleming's room, a slightly longer one, hoping that weird, snuffly Elvin had calmed down and wouldn't feel the need to whisper "behind" the moment Abby opened the door.

As she passed the office of Miss March, the nurse that Darcy and Maureen still claimed could be a star out in Hollywood, the door had opened suddenly and, to Abby's great surprise, her father, looking cheerful, had stepped out into the hallway, followed by the glamorous Helen March herself.

"Pop!" Abby had exclaimed. "What are you doing here? Is Rose okay? I just saw her. She —"

"Rose is fine," Pop had said. "Um . . ." He put his hand to his head, felt around for his hat, found that he was holding his hat in his other hand, put the hat on, then took it off again.

"Pop?" said Abby.

Her father had gripped the hat firmly in both hands. "I was just dropping off a form . . . a form for . . . I forgot to hand it in earlier." Pop had begun backing down the hallway. "Don't be late tonight," he said.

"Okay," replied Abby as Miss March scurried back inside her office.

Abby had peered after her, taken a last look at her father, and nearly reached Mr. Fleming's room when she'd felt a hand on her shoulder. She spun around to find Wyman.

"I thought you were Pop!" she'd exclaimed.

Wyman had frowned. "What?" He shook his head. "Sorry. It's just that I've been wanting to ask you something, and I didn't expect to run into you."

"I'm supposed to be in class," Abby had said, glancing at the doorway. Beyond it she could see Mr. Fleming, who was writing busily at the chalkboard.

"But I wanted to know if you'd go to the Valentine Dance with me," Wyman had whispered. "I mean, would you like to go with me?"

Abby, who had harbored a secret but futile wish that the very cute Richard Lord would invite her to the dance, smiled at Wyman and, after a pause that she hoped was too brief for him to have noticed, said, "Thank you. I'd love to go."

"Really? That's great. I'll see you after school, okay? Wait for me by the front door."

When the last class of the day had ended and Abby was bundling herself into her coat, hat, and muff — standing uncomfortably with Darcy and Maureen, who were putting on their own shabby and considerably thinner coats, and who had neither hats nor gloves, let alone muffs — Wyman had appeared at her side.

"Walk you home?" he'd asked.

Abby had glanced at Darcy, who'd raised her eyebrows, and at Maureen, who'd given her a sly smile. Then she and Wyman drifted into the crowd of students leaving school.

"Want to stop at Drugs and get a soda?" asked Wyman as he and Abby, arm in arm, had walked through town.

"I can't," Abby said with a sigh. "Now that Mama's gone, Pop keeps a closer eye on me than ever."

"Isn't your father at work now?" Wyman had asked.

"Yes. But he always finds out what's going on. You won't even be able to walk me to the house. We'll have to say good-bye at the corner. And we probably shouldn't be walking so close to each other." She'd withdrawn her arm from Wyman's elbow.

"Oh," he'd said. "Okay."

At the corner of Haddon Road, Abby had given Wyman a little wave. "Thanks for asking me to the dance. I guess I'll see you tomorrow."

Wyman lit up. "Sure! See you tomorrow."

When Abby had reached her house, she climbed the steps to the porch and opened the letter box. She'd pulled out a handful of mail and glanced through it before she went inside. Two bills, a Florida postcard from Aunt Betty and Uncle Marshall, and a letter with no return address on it, Abby's name written in the distinctive handwriting that belonged to Orrin Umhay.

She had ripped the letter open. How could Orrin have done this? What if Pop had seen the mail first? With shaking hands, she had let herself inside, tossed the rest of the mail on a table in the parlor, and run upstairs to her room. She'd closed the door and lain on her bed, the letter before her.

Dear Abby, it had begun.

I hope you arent mad. I couldnt figure out how to write to you now that your mother is gone.

Abby had rolled over on her back and stared at the ceiling. The things she missed about her mother surprised her every single day. The sight of her mother watering the rose-bushes. The sound of her mother's voice calling to her and Rose and Adele in the cottage. Very, very simple things — her mother tying Adele's shoelaces while Adele wiggled and whined and wagged her feet back and forth.

When first-term grades had been handed out just before Christmas vacation and Abby had earned straight As, her very first excited thought had been, *I have to tell Mama!* Half a second later, as she remembered that Mama was gone, Abby had felt chilled. How could she *not* have remembered such a thing? Maybe something was wrong with her.

And now this letter from Orrin. Ever since Sarah had died, Orrin had managed to write to Abby by mailing his letters to Mama with various vague return addresses that Pop wouldn't question if he saw the envelopes. Mama had known whom the letters were actually for and whom they were actually from, and had slipped them under Abby's pillow before Pop could see them.

But in August, panicked and frightened after her mother's funeral, Abby had written Orrin a hasty note and mailed it from the post office, telling him that they would have to find some other way for him to write to her. She had sent him four more letters after that and hadn't heard from him, until that very moment.

I am so sorry about your mother. My parents send their condolances too. What should we do about writing. I like getting your letters but I want to write to you too and I dont know where to send them. I hope you dont get into trouble because of this letter. Well we'll figure something out.

Here is good news. Ma and Pap and I are going to visit Lewisport this summer. I hope we can see each other and talk in person. I know it will have to be in secret, I guess thats okay.

You must be very sad now but this will be something to look forward to. Tell me what you think in your next letter.

Abby had skipped to the end of the page where Orrin had signed his note, as always, *Your Orrin*. Below that he'd added a postscript: *P.S. I can drive now! You give me any kind of car and I can drive it.*

Abby had smiled. She'd just added the letter to the stack that she hid in a box in her closet, when she'd heard the doorbell ring. A moment later Rose's voice called from below, "Abby, your sweetheart is here!"

"Rose!"

"You'd better come downstairs before he runs away."

"Rose, get up here," Abby had whispered loudly, and when Rose stuck her head in the room, Abby said, "*Who* is here?"

"Your boyfriend Zander."

"Zander? What's he doing home?"

Rose had shrugged dramatically. "I never heard anyone ask so many questions. Just go downstairs. He came over to see you."

Abby, flushing pink and breathing fast, had run downstairs. "Hi!" she'd squeaked when she saw Zander Burley. His height had surprised her. He'd seemed taller than ever. His Adam's apple was now exactly at her eye level. Did boys continue to grow even when they were in college? Boys were very mysterious creatures.

Abby had tried to lower her voice. "I didn't think you were going to be back until the end of the term." Zander was halfway through his second year at Harvard.

"I'm taking a couple of days off," he'd said.

"Well, won't you —" Abby hesitated. She'd been about to invite Zander inside, but if letting Wyman near the house wasn't allowed, then surely letting Zander all the way into the parlor would have been a huge mistake, no matter how highly her father thought of Mr. Burley.

Zander had waved her off. "Thanks, but I can't stay. I just wanted to tell you that I'll be back the weekend of your Valentine's Day dance and I wondered if I could be your escort."

"You want to take *me*? To the *high school* dance?"

Zander had grinned. "Sure. I miss the place. I'd like to see the old crowd."

Abby could feel herself flushing again. "I wish I could go with you. It's just that someone . . . Do you know Wyman Todd? He asked me to go with him. But," she had continued hastily, seeing the disappointment on Zander's face, "you should go to the dance anyway. Everyone would love to see you. And I can't dance *every* dance with Wyman." She'd smiled.

Zander had smiled back in his lazy way. He didn't look so owlish anymore, Abby had thought. He was confident and sturdy and he grinned easily. "I think I will go," he'd said. "Wear a red rose in your hair, all right, Abby?" He'd turned to leave.

Abby had closed the door softly behind Zander and returned to her bedroom. Two invitations to the dance and a letter from Orrin, all in one afternoon. It had been exactly the kind of day she wished she could tell Mama about.

And now it was seven o'clock on the night of February 11th. The dance would start in an hour, and Abby had to choose her jewelry and decide how to wear the rose and . . .

"Adele? Do I have too much perfume on?"

Adele sniffed the air and shrugged.

"Go out in the hall and see if you can smell —"

The doorbell rang.

"Ooh, Abby, it's Wy-man!" Rose sang from below.

Abby stuck Zander's flower behind her ear again (this time it stayed put), and decided there was nothing more to be done about her appearance. She turned off her light, walked down the stairs in as elegant a manner as she could muster, and found Wyman standing nervously in the hallway, holding out a box containing a single red rose.

"Oh!" exclaimed Wyman. "You already have a rose."

Abby could feel herself blushing. "I'll — I'll pin yours on my dress," she stammered, before Wyman could ask where the rose in her hair had come from.

She did so, then kissed Pop on the forehead.

"Be home by ten o'clock," he said firmly.

The gymnasium at BPCH had been transformed. When Abby entered it, her arm hooked through Wyman's, she felt her breath catch. "It's beautiful," she whispered.

Red hearts of all sizes fluttered just below the ceiling. Red and silver streamers crisscrossed the room. Wooden cupids, painstakingly fashioned by one of the art classes, stood at either end of the refreshments table, which held a glass bowl full of red punch and an array of red cakes and cookies. Helen March and Madame Ponsin, the French teacher, were smiling and ladling punch into cups. Abby looked around at the students, who had been equally transformed since she had seen them the day before. Gone were the plaid skirts and saddle shoes and bobby socks. Gone were the letterman jackets and loafers. In their places were red gowns and full-skirted dresses, suits and jackets and ties.

"May I have this dance?" Wyman asked, and he swung Abby onto the dance floor. They swirled past Maureen, who was in the arms of Richard Lord. When she was facing Abby, Maureen pointed to the back of Richard's handsome head and made the thumbs-up sign. They swirled past Darcy, who was dancing with Elvin Burrows and who, when *she* was facing Abby, crossed her eyes and smacked herself on the side of her head.

Abby, her arms wrapped around Wyman's neck, was struggling not to laugh when Wyman suddenly came to a stop. She heard him say, "What?"

She let go of Wyman and turned around.

"I asked if I could cut in," Zander Burley was saying. He paused. "Abby, you have *two* roses."

"What?" said Wyman again.

"What?" said Abby.

Wyman and Zander frowned at each other.

"Do you mind if I dance with Zander?" Abby asked Wyman.

Wyman shrugged.

"You can have the next dance," she told him, feeling generous. And soon she was swirling around the gym with Zander.

This was how she spent much of the evening: Zander cutting in on Wyman, Wyman cutting in on Zander.

At last she said to Wyman, "I'm tired! Can we go get some punch?"

They found a long line at the refreshments table and Wyman groaned. Then to Abby's surprise, a cup of punch was pressed into her hand, and she looked up into the face of Helen March.

"Hi, Abby!" exclaimed Miss March. "I'll bet you need this. Are you having fun?"

"Um, yes." Abby glanced at Wyman and raised her eyebrows.

"You look lovely," Miss March went on, and suddenly Abby wanted to cry. She had longed to hear those words all night, had longed for her mother to take her by the shoulders and look into her eyes and say that she would surely be the most beautiful girl at the dance.

And now here was the school nurse telling her she looked lovely.

"Thanks," Abby replied, and found herself supremely grateful when, moments later, Zander once again approached her, and soon they were rocking back and forth in each other's arms, as if they were the only two people in the gym.

Chapter 17

Saturday, September 9th, 1939

It was wrong, Abby thought. It was so very, very wrong.

Helen March was only six years older than Abby. *Six years.*

Abby awoke half an hour before her alarm clock went off, and she was glad. She probably hadn't allowed enough time for all the preparations that would be needed that morning. She ran down the hall to Adele's room, knocking on Rose's door on the way. "Get up, Rose!" she called.

She peeked into Adele's room, which was stuffy and littered with dolls and discarded doll clothes. "Adele," she said, "time to wake up."

"No, it isn't," said Adele from under a mound of covers and a pile of naked baby dolls.

"Yes, it is. We have a lot to do this morning."

"No, we don't."

"Yes, we do. It's a big day."

"No, it isn't."

"Adele."

"No!"

"You have a new dress, and yesterday I got a pink ribbon for your hair."

"No, you di — A pink ribbon?"

Abby withdrew it from the pocket of her dressing gown. "Here it is. You are going to be the most gorgeous four-year-old at the wedding."

"Four-and-a-half-year-old."

"Yes. The most gorgeous four-and-a-half-year-old at the wedding."

"I'm the flower girl."

"Right. And that's why you need to get up now. You need to eat breakfast and have a bath. Then I'm going to curl your hair, and you'll get dressed. Rose and I have to get ready, too. We have to look perfect for Pop."

Adele slid out of her bed. "Can the dollies come to the wedding with me?"

"Not all of them."

"One dolly?"

"If you put some clothes on her."

"Okay. I choose" — Adele pawed through the dolls — "Shirley." She selected a curly-headed doll and dressed her in a red sweater and a flared pink skating skirt. "There."

"Wonderful. Now come on downstairs. Ellen's fixing breakfast."

The morning was spent in a whirl of bathing and hair curling and fussing in front of the mirror, and then of buttoning buttons and tying sashes and straightening lace flowers under the critical eyes of Sheila.

Abby and Rose were facing each other in the bathroom, Abby adjusting Rose's collar and Rose combing Abby's hair, when a knock came on the door.

"We have to leave in half an hour, girls," Pop warned them.

"Okay!" they chimed out.

Abby waited until Pop's footsteps had retreated down the hall. "Try to smile today, Rose," she said quietly. "For Adele's sake, if no one else's. She's so excited about her dress." Rose made a face. "Just *try*," said Abby again. "We can't look like sourpusses in front of Aunt Betty and Uncle Marshall either."

"I'm surprised they're even coming."

"They're coming for us. But they aren't going to go to the reception."

"I don't blame them. Anyway, you have to try to smile, too," said Rose.

"I will."

"Just think of one of your many beaus."

"Very funny," said Abby, but she blushed as she recalled her secret visit with Orrin. They'd spent an afternoon together when the Umhays had returned to Lewisport six weeks earlier. A single afternoon that had slipped by like a minute: an afternoon of sitting on the rocks at the far end of the beach, the pine forest at their backs, the sun warming their skin.

"Remember clamming?" Abby had said.

"Remember the fair?"

"Remember hide-and-seek with Sarah?"

And soon the sun was dropping behind the trees and their visit was over. But already the letters had started, and now Orrin wrote as many as Abby did, sending his letters to Maureen, since she was always the first to get the mail at her house, and she gave them to Abby in school the next day.

Zander, in the meantime, never wrote. He'd kissed the top of her head after their last dance on that wondrous night in February, and he'd called hello to her from next door several times over the summer, but while he was a writer (or planned to be one), he was not, he'd mentioned to her rather casually, a letter writer.

"All right," said Abby, turning away from Rose to check herself in the mirror. "I think we're ready."

* * *

Adele chattered all the way from Haddon Road to the church, seated primly in the back of the car with Rose and Abby, Shirley in her lap.

"Pop," she called to the front seat, where her father was sitting next to Mike, "thank you for this dress. Abby said I will be the most gorgeous four-and-a-half-year-old at the wedding."

"Sure thing," said Pop.

"I brought Shirley with me," she went on. "She has clothes on. Can I wear my flower-girl dress to church tomorrow? Sheila said to be sure to keep the dress clean. I won't spill on it, I promise." And on and on.

When Mike parked in front of the church at the other end of Barnegat Point, Abby thought the street seemed unusually quiet. "You'd never know there was going to be a wedding here in half an hour," she whispered to Rose.

Rose shrugged and rolled her eyes.

The little stone church was cool inside, cool but bright. Sun shone through the windows and slanted across the floor. The lone stained-glass window laid bars of red and blue and purple along the front two pews.

"Look! I turned into a plum!" exclaimed Adele, sticking her hand in a shaft of purple light.

"*Shh,*" said Pop. "We're in church."

The wedding began promptly at eleven-thirty. Scattered throughout the pews were Aunt Betty and Uncle Marshall, several of Pop's workers and their wives, Ellen, Sheila, and Mike, and several people Abby didn't recognize. Abby and Rose stood woodenly at the front of the church with Pop, clutching bouquets of lilies. Abby's hands began to shake and the lilies vibrated until Rose placed her hand over hers and held on tight.

There was a small clatter at the back then, and Adele appeared in her finery, holding a basket of rose petals, which she scattered from right to left as she made her way down the aisle. Abby could see the top of Shirley's head in the basket. As Adele passed Aunt Betty, she paused, twirled around, and said, "Do you like my dress?"

Abby heard gentle laughter and beckoned Adele forward. When the three sisters were standing together, Abby's hands resting on Adele's shoulders, there was an expectant hush and the wedding guests turned to look at the back of the church. The organ, which had been wheezing out "Nearer, My God, to Thee," paused, and as the first few notes of Mendelssohn's "Wedding March" sounded, the bride made her way up the aisle, smiling nervously, her father holding her elbow.

They reached the front, the bride's father stepped away, and Pop and Helen March gazed into each other's eyes.

Abby pursed her lips and fought back a sob.

The reception was held at home. Mike hurried Ellen and Sheila back to the house the moment the wedding was over, and then returned to the church for Pop and Helen. Abby, Rose, and Adele rode with their aunt and uncle; Abby and Rose said nothing during the short ride to Haddon, although Adele continued chattering, this time about wedding gowns and rings and how well she had done in her vital role as flower girl.

"Maybe *we* can skip the party, too," Rose whispered to Abby as they climbed the porch steps a few minutes later and watched Uncle Marshall and Aunt Betty drive off.

Abby shook her head. "Pop would kill us."

"Did you notice that Helen's father looks exactly the same age as Pop?"

"Yes," said Abby dully.

Abby plopped down on a corner of the sofa in the parlor and didn't get up until the last guest had left. "Come on, Adele. Let's change out of our dresses," she said, extending her hand to her little sister.

"No! I don't want to take mine off."

"Well, you have to."

"No! Sheila will let me leave it on."

"Adele?" Helen was standing in the hallway. "You really do have to take your dress off. Look. I took my wedding gown off. It's time to put the fancy dresses away. And then you need to take a nap."

"A nap?" said Adele.

"Adele doesn't take naps anymore," said Abby.

"All four-year-olds take naps," Helen replied.

"I'm four and a *half.*"

"Nap," Helen said firmly.

"You're not in charge of me."

"I'm your mother now." Helen said this mildly, but Abby thought her eyes looked sharp.

"You're our stepmother," Abby pointed out.

"Go upstairs and take your dress off," Helen said to Adele. "And then lie down and take a nap."

Adele glanced at Abby and headed for the stairs. Abby followed her wordlessly. An image of Helen pressing a cup of punch into her hand at the Valentine's Day dance came to her. *Fraud*, she thought. *Hypocrite.*

The truck arrived two hours later. It backed up the driveway and parked next to the kitchen entrance, one of the movers leaping out before the motor had been turned off. Pop met him at the door.

"Where do you want everything?" asked the man.

Pop began giving instructions, and Abby and Rose, joined by a sleepy Adele, watched as Helen's trunks, cartons, and hatboxes were carried inside.

"What's all that?" asked Adele.

"They're Helen's things," Rose told her. "She lives here now."

"With us? Forever?"

"Yup."

Later, Adele ran up the stairs. "Abby!" she called. "Rose! Come quick! Helen is putting her clothes in Mama's dresser. And in Mama's *closet.*"

Abby followed her sister. They stood outside the room in which Adele had been born and in which, three and a half years later, Mama had died. Helen's back was toward them and she was reaching for Mama's scented coat hangers, a pile of blouses over her arm.

Adele tugged at Abby's sleeve and led her down the hall. "But is she really our mama?" she whispered.

"No."

"So what do we call her?"

"I'm going to call her Helen."

Adele looked thoughtful. "Maybe I'll call her Mama Helen," she said after a moment.

Abby felt her stomach drop away. Adele, she realized, would remember no mother other than Helen March.

Chapter 18

Abby slid into her seat at the breakfast table, picked up her napkin, and underneath, found a slim blue box tied with a white satin ribbon.

"What's this?" she asked, smiling.

Pop and Helen smiled back at her.

"Open it," said Pop.

"It's for our graduate," added Helen.

"I have a present for you, too!" exclaimed Adele, who was seated across the table from Abby, perched on a dictionary. "I made it myself." She handed her sister a large piece of folded paper.

"Thanks," said Abby.

Rose, who had been in a bad mood practically since the day of Pop's wedding, said, "I didn't know we were supposed to get you presents," and returned to her oatmeal.

"That's okay." Abby opened Adele's picture first. "It's beautiful!" she exclaimed.

"I painted it without any help at all. Do you know what it is?"

"Well . . ." said Abby.

"It's Santa Claus," Adele informed her. "Because Santa Claus is nice and I wanted to paint you something nice for your gradulations."

"Thank you very much." Abby set the painting aside and pulled the ribbon off the blue box. Inside was a pen and pencil set, a black pen and a black pencil, each trimmed in gold leaf. "They're lovely," said Abby, who knew that even Darcy's parents, poor as they were, had gotten their daughter a locket with her initial on it to wear around her neck. And that Maureen's parents had presented her with a school days memory book. Personal presents from parents who knew their daughters well.

Then Pop said, "For our writer," and Abby suddenly felt both petty and pleased.

"Thank you," she said, her voice barely above a whisper. Laughing, she added, "I'll write my first book with them."

"Girls can't be writers," said Rose, from the other end of the table.

"Of course they can be. What about Emily Brontë? And Pearl Buck?"

"Don't you have to go to college to be a writer?"

Abby sighed. It was enough that Pop thought she might become a writer. She wasn't going to ask him about college again. "Girls don't need college," he had said many times.

"Well, then why are there women's colleges?" Abby once asked him.

"Why are there lots of things?" Pop had countered. "Why are there synagogues? Why are there colleges for Negroes? Just because they exist doesn't mean we need them."

Abby knew it was pointless to argue with him about such things, no matter how badly she wanted to.

She turned to Rose. "Lots of famous writers didn't go to college. They write from experience, from the heart. Anyway, I'd better get going. I don't want to miss a single thing at school today. Remember, graduation starts at two this afternoon. You should get to the auditorium early if you want good seats." (Helen no longer worked at Barnegat Point Central High. She no longer worked at all.)

Abby hurried out the door and along Haddon to the corner where Darcy and Maureen were waiting for her.

"Can you believe it?" asked Maureen, and she threw her arms around Abby.

"Graduation at last," Abby replied.

"One more day and then we can get on with the rest of our lives," said Darcy.

"That's easy for you to say. You know what the rest of your life is going to be. I don't."

Darcy held out her hand and once again showed off the promise ring that Arthur Scovil had given her two weeks earlier.

"You're so lucky," said Maureen.

"So are you!" Abby exclaimed, turning to Maureen. "You got a job with the phone company, just like you wanted."

"I know. But I want to get married, too. I want babies. And I haven't met the right boy yet. This time next year Darcy will probably be married with a baby on the way. I don't want to wait too long."

Abby sighed. What she really wanted was to go to college. And what Pop really wanted was for her not to go to college, and instead to marry a nice rich man and settle down in Barnegat Point. Maybe that wouldn't be so bad, thought Abby. But in the meantime, while she was finding the nice rich man and not going to college, the least she could do was get a job and work, like Maureen. But Pop had nixed that idea, too.

The girls walked through town, and when Barnegat Point Central High came into view, Abby found that there were tears in her eyes. This, she realized, was the last day, the absolute last day, that she would be a student. Year after year, since she was six and living in Lewisport, her time had been structured around school. Around tests and classes and projects and vacations. Now it was over and she was being thrust into the adult world. But someone had forgotten to give her a compass.

"Abby?" said Darcy. "What are you waiting for? Come on. Hey, you're not crying, are you? You big baby! Let's get going."

Abby cheered up when she and her friends entered the school and were directed to a table outside the principal's office, where the commencement-days souvenir books were being given out to the students.

Abby accepted hers and stared at the cover: It was creamy white with *Commencement Days* written in fancy blue script above a red rose. She opened it. The first page was headed: Class of 19__. Underneath were spaces in which to record her name, the class officers, class flower, class motto, and class cheer. She walked outside with her friends and they sat in the grass. Carefully they filled in the blank with "40," and then began to write.

"Oh, look at the next page," said Maureen. "Autographs. Let's start collecting them. You write in mine first, Abby."

The girls exchanged books. In Maureen's, Abby wrote, Blessed are those who sit on tacks, for they shall rise immediately. In

Darcy's, she wrote, *Ashes to ashes, dust to dust, if it weren't for BPCH, our brains would rust.*

Other students joined them and soon the books were being passed from hand to hand to hand and the autographs were flowing.

2 good 2 B 4-got.
4-get me not.
Best wishes for your future.
Remember Grant, remember Lee, forget them all — remember me.

The next few hours were spent cleaning out desks and asking teachers to sign the souvenir books and eating lunch on the school lawn. At last it was time for the students to go to the gymnasium and put on their caps and gowns.

"I know I've been saying this all day," Abby said to Maureen as she adjusted the sleeves of her gown, "but —"

"But I can't believe we're graduating!" Maureen finished for her.

"Actually, I was going to say — again — that I can't believe this day is here. But I guess that's the same thing. Remember when we met each other, freshman year? Doesn't that seem like just a few months ago? Even first grade could be just a few months ago. How did it all go by so fast? And now you have a job and Darcy has her promise ring. Adele will turn six on her next birthday."

"Did you hear that Richard Lord enlisted in the army?" Darcy spoke up.

"Really?" said Abby. "But America hasn't entered the war. We declared neutrality."

"We'll be in it soon enough. You know that," said Maureen. "My brother told me that our government just approved the sale of surplus war material to Great Britain. That's kind of like taking sides, isn't it?"

Abby nodded. It was, although she didn't like to think about the war. She also knew that Richard wasn't the only BPCH senior who had enlisted in the army.

"I don't want to be eighteen," she said suddenly. "I want to be Adele's age again."

She felt tears spring to her eyes, but before they could spill over, she heard the booming voice of Mr. Cantwell, the vice principal, as he clapped his hands for attention.

"Seniors, you should have your caps and gowns now. Please follow me to the auditorium. It's time for the program to begin."

The seniors jostled themselves into line in alphabetical order, as they had practiced the day before. Abby glanced behind her at Maureen and Darcy, who were nearby. She gave them a wave, and then the students proceeded down the hall and into the auditorium, which was abuzz with the chatter of parents and grandparents and brothers and sisters. They filed onto the stage and Abby took her seat and stared out into the audience until she spotted Pop, Helen, Rose, and Adele. Adele was waving madly at Abby and wouldn't stop until Rose swatted her with her accordion fan.

A hush descended on the auditorium and Abby allowed herself a small fantasy. She squinted her eyes and pretended that instead of Pop, Helen, Rose, and Adele in the sixth row, she saw Pop, Mama, Rose, Adele, and, squirming in Mama's lap, Fred. In her fantasy, Mama looked pink cheeked and she was smiling broadly. And Fred was not only taller but sturdier, sitting up straight, calling, "Abby! Hi, Abby!"

Then she pretended that two seats away from her, next to Angela Michaels, was Sarah Moreside, grinning at her proud parents, who were seated behind Mama and Pop.

Abby shook her head. She felt tears once again, and she blinked her eyes furiously, determined not to cry. When she heard the squeal of a microphone, she straightened herself and looked defiantly at the audience. The program had begun.

The principal welcomed the students and guests. Harley Eaton, the class president, gave a speech entitled "Looking to the Future." Marlene Fitzsimmons sang a solo, "A Brown Bird Singing." When prizes were awarded, Abby won Overall Academic Achievement and her classmates cheered as she accepted her plaque.

And then . . . diplomas were handed out, Marlene sang "America the Beautiful," and the student orchestra played "The Graduation March" while the seniors filed back off the stage, diplomas in hand.

Graduation was over.

"We did it!" Darcy cried as the seniors ran out onto the school lawn. "It's over! We made it!" She tossed her cap in the air.

Abby hugged her friends fiercely. Parents trickled out of the school building, and children ran in wild zigzags, laughing, hiding behind graduation gowns, and begging the photographer to take their pictures. Abby had just caught sight of Pop and Helen when someone tapped her shoulder, and she turned around.

"Zander! What are you doing here?"

"I came to watch you graduate. Congratulations, Abby. Nice job getting the top prize."

Abby grinned. "I don't know what I'm going to do with it, though. Or with my diploma, for that matter."

He grinned back. "You'll think of something."

Adele launched herself at Abby then, and suddenly Abby was surrounded by her family, and then by a raucous group of students: Wyman, Darcy, Maureen, kids from the annual and *Words* and *In Our Voices*.

The photographer hurried across the lawn and took a picture of them, which wound up in the Barnegat Point *Record* the next week. Abby felt jubilant.

Then the afternoon ended and her friends scattered and Abby walked home with her family, clutching her diploma and wondering what she was going to do with the rest of her life.

Chapter 19

Thursday, August 1st, 1940

"Good-bye," Abby said quietly over her shoulder to Miss Doris as she left the Barnegat Point library. "I'll see you tomorrow."

Miss Doris gave Abby a finger wave and whispered, "Bye." As head librarian, Miss Doris felt she must always honor her own rule of no talking in the library, unless speaking *in a whisper* to one of the other librarians.

Abby stepped out into the heat and fanned herself with the magazine Miss Doris had let her take home. That was one of the nice things about her job at the library: She got to bring home all sorts of new books and magazines before anyone else saw them, as long as she returned them when she arrived at the library the next morning.

Abby walked slowly along the main street through town. She still marveled that Pop had relented and allowed her to look for a job.

"A *respectable* job," he had said firmly. In other words, Abby was not allowed to work as a waitress or at the movie theatre or behind the counter at Miss Maynard's store. In fact, he didn't want her working at any store. "You're not supposed to look like you need a job," he had told her. "How about seeing if Miss Doris needs help at the library? That would be nice, genteel work for a young girl."

Abby had sighed, although in truth she'd liked the idea of working at the library. She would be surrounded by books all day long. She could read to little children and see new books when they came in, and at the end of her shift, she could check out books about writing and the great poets.

A month after she had graduated, Abby, dressed in one of her church dresses and a hat that she felt Mama would have approved of, had approached Miss Doris at the library, and half an hour later had been offered a job.

"Part-time," Miss Doris had told her. "Five mornings a week. But at the end of the summer I'll reconsider. I may have an opening for a full-time employee then."

Employee. Abby loved the word. She had gotten her way. Sort of. She wasn't a college student, but she wasn't sitting around Barnegat Point waiting for a husband to appear at her door either.

Abby continued languidly down the street. At Allie's, a café that had opened at the beginning of the summer, she took a seat at a tiny table by the door and ordered a cup of coffee and a sandwich, feeling supremely grown-up. She paid for the food with her own money — not Pop's — and sat and read the magazine. When she was finished with her lunch, she tipped Allie and walked the rest of the way home, humming under her breath.

"Hello!" she called as she entered her house. The windows were flung wide open against the heat, and a fan was turning in the parlor. "Where is everyone?" she called. She had seen Adele's abandoned crayons and a Shirley Temple coloring book on the porch, but no sign of Adele or anyone else.

"Hello?" she called again.

"Abby, please, I was trying to nap." Helen's voice floated crankily to Abby from upstairs. Presently she appeared on the landing, hands cradling the roundness that would soon produce Abby's new little brother or sister.

"Well, you didn't have to get out of bed," Abby snapped. "I didn't know you were asleep. I was just wondering where everyone was."

"All you had to do was go in the kitchen and ask Ellen."

"Fine," said Abby, the contentment of the day washing away. She huffed into the kitchen and sat down at the table.

"I will be so glad when she finally has that baby" was the first thing she said to Ellen. "Three more months. How are we all going to stand it?"

Ellen smiled. "You're as cranky as she is."

"Sorry. She makes me so mad. According to her, I never do anything right. I'm rude and thoughtless and stubborn and —"

"Don't listen to her."

Abby made a face. "Where are Rose and Adele?"

"Rose took Adele down the street to play with Bertie. They'll be back later."

Abby tiptoed upstairs to her room and lay on her bed. Eighteen years old and she was still living at home in a room with dolls on the shelves. Darcy had quietly gotten married to Arthur a month earlier, and they had moved to their very own house, a tiny cottage outside of Lewisport. And Maureen, whose job at the phone company was going well, had moved to a room in a boarding house in St. George. At least once a week, Zander, who was working at the offices of the *Record* that summer, would call for Abby and they would go to a movie or maybe take a ride in his fancy new car, but Abby felt like an infant compared to her friends. She was grateful to be able to go to the library every morning, and she liked getting a paycheck, but when she returned to the house on

Haddon and entered her room, she felt like a little girl again. A little girl without very much to do.

She was skimming the last page of the magazine later when she heard Pop's car in the drive and, not long after that, his rapid knock on her door.

"Abby?"

Abby tensed. Had Helen already told him about their argument?

"Come in." She sat up, patting her hair into place.

Pop stepped inside and perched on the edge of the bed. He was smiling. "I have some wonderful news." He sounded very pleased with himself. "Guess who stopped by the shop this afternoon."

Abby shook her head. "I don't know. Who?"

"Zander."

Abby wasn't sure what she was supposed to say to this, so she said nothing.

"He isn't going to be here much longer, you know."

Abby looked sharply at Pop. "What do you mean?"

"Zander," he said, "has enlisted in the army."

"What?" cried Abby. Zander hadn't said anything about the army to her.

"He'll be shipping out in three weeks."

Abby almost exclaimed, "Oh no!" But Pop was a firm believer in the United States Army and enjoyed watching America flex its muscles, so she lay back on her pillows and again said nothing.

"That isn't the wonderful news, though," said Pop. "The wonderful news is that Zander has asked for your hand in marriage."

For a moment, Abby simply stared. "My hand?" she said finally. "Zander wants to *marry* me? Marry *me*?" And then she added, "Now? He hasn't even graduated from college yet."

Abby couldn't remember a time since moving to Barnegat Point that Zander hadn't been part of her life. Not in the way that Rose or Adele or Maureen or Darcy had been part of her life. With Zander it was different. He was always *there* somehow, even when he wasn't actually present. Abby was aware of Zander, whether she was watching him from her bedroom window or dancing with him at the Valentine Dance or thinking of him working away at Harvard while she plowed through her high school homework. When she wrote a story or a poem, she could hear Zander critiquing it as she worked.

Certainly Zander was cute. Darcy had pointed that out many, many times. In fact, he was more than cute. Once he had moved past his scrawny phase, he'd grown into the kind of boy who all the girls wanted to be seen with. He was handsome and smart and . . . exciting. He was so exciting that Abby was a little surprised that Pop still held him in such high esteem. Zander drove his car too fast, and he liked alcohol. A lot. Pop, who never drank, had made remarks about Zander's alcohol consumption. But when you got right down to it, Zander was still a Burley, the son of the richest man in Barnegat Point, and that meant a lot to Luther Nichols.

"Zander wants to marry *me*?" Abby couldn't help saying again. She and Zander had spent more time together than usual that summer, but they hadn't discussed marriage.

"He does," said Pop solemnly. "And he's the only boy I can think of who's worthy of you. A Burley-Nichols match. Now, it may be that you'll want to have the wedding after he comes back from Europe, but it makes much more sense to have it right away, before he leaves."

"Pop!" exclaimed Abby. What she wanted to say to him was "You can't make my decisions for me." What came out of her mouth instead was "I don't want to marry Zander," although she wasn't sure that was true.

Pop's face darkened. "Abigail, if Zander Burley asks for your hand in marriage, then you accept. I have to be able to hold my head up in this town."

"But, Pop —"

"This isn't open to argument. This isn't a suggestion. I'm telling you that Zander has asked to marry you, and so you are going to marry him." He frowned at her. "I thought you'd be happy."

"I am. I like Zander. But I like Wyman and Richard, too."

"I don't see them coming around with proposals. More important, Abby, if you and Zander marry, you'll never have to worry about money. You can have the perfect life here. The best of the best of everything. Now you go next door. Zander is waiting for your answer."

"I'm supposed to go over there right now?"

Pop sighed. "Look, if you want to wait until after he's back from Europe to have the wedding, that would be all right. But you have to accept his proposal now."

He left the room then and Abby knelt at her window. She tried to see into Zander's room, and she wondered what the Burleys would do with his room once he shipped out. Then she stood for a long time in front of her mirror, looking at her eighteen-year-old Barnegat Point self and seeing instead her five-year-old Lewisport self. What would Mama say to her if she were here? Would what she said matter? Mama had never stood up to Pop.

Abby changed into a clean dress, brushed her hair, and

walked slowly down the stairs to the front hall. She met Rose and Adele on her way out.

"Where are you going?" asked Rose.

"Nowhere. I'll see you later."

Abby's heart began to pound as she crossed her yard to the Burleys'. By the time she reached their front porch, her hands were shaking so badly she could barely ring the bell.

Zander answered the door, a shy smile on his face. He beckoned her inside. "Let's go sit down," he said, and led her into the parlor. He closed the door behind them and looked at her expectantly, taking her hands in his as he pulled her onto the sofa.

Abby offered him a smile. "Pop just told me," she said. "I can't believe it."

"I know it's sudden. But, Abby, I think I've been in love with you since the day we met." Zander blushed. "And when I found out how soon I'd be going overseas, I didn't want to wait any longer to ask you."

"Pop wants us to get married right away," said Abby. "Before you leave."

"That was my idea," said Zander.

Abby drew in her breath. "I can't do it."

"You want to wait?"

Abby shook her head. "No."

"What are you saying?"

"I'm saying that I can't marry you."

Zander dropped his hands to his lap.

"It just doesn't feel right. I'm sorry." Abby kissed Zander's cheek. Then she rose and let herself out. She stood on the Burleys' porch and looked at her own house. The light was fading and Ellen had turned on a lamp in the parlor. Abby could see Adele, her head bent over her coloring book. Helen was standing by the fireplace, talking to Pop.

Abby turned right and walked down Haddon Road. She needed to think before she faced her father.

She knew what she'd done. She knew what this meant.

She could leave Barnegat Point. She would have to leave.

It was time to say good-bye.

Epilogue

Wednesday, February 14th, 1945

"Bye, Sylvie. Bye, Jean. Bye, Martha." Abby fastened her new velvet hat to her head with a complicated arrangement of bobby pins and let herself out of Fosgood's, a temporary-job placement agency. She waited for the elevator to arrive at the fourth floor, mentally listing the things she needed to do that evening. *Buy a pork chop for dinner*, she was thinking, when a hand caught her elbow.

"Come out for a coffee with June and me before you go home?" asked Edie Matthews. "We've hardly seen you this week."

"Mr. Fosgood keeps dumping files on my desk," said Abby. "Huge files. I've hardly had a spare moment since Monday."

"So come with us. We're going to Schrafft's."

Abby sighed. "I'd like to, but that's all the way downtown. I've got to get home. Take a rain check? Maybe on Friday?"

"All right. See you tomorrow, Abby."

Abby stepped out into the chilly, damp air of a February evening in New York City and began the walk from Forty-Eighth Street to Sixty-Third Street. Her purse clutched tightly in one hand, she hurried along among the crowds of people who were rushing home or running errands, always hurrying, hurrying.

Nothing in Barnegat Point could have prepared Abby for Manhattan. She had never encountered so many people moving so fast. New Yorkers, it seemed, never did anything slowly. Rush, rush, rush. Rush from home to work to the store to the theatre to a museum. Abby loved every second of every day with its *rat-a-tat* rhythm. When Rose wrote letters from home, she wanted all the details of Abby's glamorous life.

"It isn't glamorous," Abby had told her on one of their rare phone calls. "I work for a temp agency. I live in a two-room third-floor walk-up and I don't have a telephone."

"But you're on your own. You have a job. You're in the middle of the greatest city in the world. You see famous people walking down the street." (Abby had once glimpsed Richard Widmark in a delicatessen on Broadway.)

Abby had laughed. "It is fun," she'd agreed. "Yesterday Edie and I took a carriage ride through Central Park."

"Oh, that sounds wonderful!"

"It was. I felt like we were in a movie. Oh, and I'm going to have another poem published!"

"Abby, you're famous!"

"Not yet. Three poems and two short stories. I'm not famous. But it is exciting. Look, I have to go. I'm using Nate's phone again, and he's not even charging me. Kiss Harry and Teddy for me. And say hi to Adele the next time you see her. Bye!"

Now Abby continued on her way home, stopping her hurrying long enough to duck into the butcher's and buy the pork chop. Two blocks later she stopped in a stationer's and bought a box of note cards. She wrote faithfully to Pop and Helen. Once a week. She knew her letters were dull, but she found it hard to muster any enthusiasm when writing to them. "How are you? How is everyone in Barnegat Point? How is Miles?" (Miles was Pop and Helen's four-year-old son, and the bane of Adele's existence, according to Adele.) "Have you been to the cottage lately? Give my love to Ellen and Sheila and Mike." Abby rarely mentioned herself or her life in Manhattan. Pop thought New York City was as evil as the devil himself, which gave Abby's life there an added charm, in her eyes, but she thought it best not to rub the fact in every time she wrote a letter. She was a young woman living alone in a city of sin, working in an office in order to pay the rent on an apartment so tiny it could probably fit in the parlor of the house on Haddon. Not to mention that her living alone reminded Pop of another disappointing fact — that Abby had declined to marry Zander. What was worse, she hadn't married at all.

Rose, on the other hand, who was just twenty, two years younger than Abby, was already married and had a little boy. And she had remained in Barnegat Point. True, she and her family had settled in the outskirts of the town, but they saw Pop and Helen and Miles and Adele several times a week. Occasionally, Abby would waken in the small hours of the morning and think longingly of her sisters and of the town in which she'd grown up — and then the sun would rise, streaking the Manhattan sky with pink and blue, and she would look out her window at the view of the coffee shop and the shoe repair store on Sixty-Third, and remember that Mr. Fosgood had given her a ticket to the ballet or that she had a date to meet the girls at Schrafft's, and her homesickness would melt into excitement over another day in the great Big Apple.

Abby, now carrying her purse, her dinner, and the box of stationery, turned the corner on to Sixty-Third Street and hustled through the fading daylight to her building. She climbed the stoop, calling hello to Mrs. Graumann who, summer or winter, spent much of each day with her bedroom window wide open, elbows resting on the sill, keeping an eye on the comings and goings of her neighbors.

"Evening, Abby," replied Mrs. Graumann. "You need a warmer coat. That's not fit for the middle of February."

"Maybe next year," said Abby.

Leaving Pop and Barnegat Point had meant doing without a lot of things Abby had become accustomed to. She had to plan carefully if she wanted to go to the beauty parlor or buy a theatre ticket — or a new winter coat. But she was on her own. She had proved to herself that she didn't need anyone to take care of her. Rose had moved from Pop's house to Harry's house with nothing in between. Abby had wanted the in-between.

"You need a beau," Mrs. Graumann said as Abby was reaching for the door. "A pretty girl like you — where are all your beaus?"

Abby shrugged and smiled and let herself into the building, calling good night over her shoulder. She began climbing the stairs and found herself thinking of Zander Burley. According to Rose, who had run into Zander several weeks earlier, he had returned safely from overseas and was visiting his family in Barnegat Point. Maybe Abby should plan a visit to Barnegat Point. Or maybe not.

At the second floor, Abby knocked on the door of apartment 2C. "It's me!" she called.

The door was opened by a slender young man with wide-set eyes and brown hair parted exactly in the middle.

"Hi, Nate," said Abby. "Is it still all right if I use your phone? Today is my little sister's birthday. I promise I won't talk long."

Nate smiled at her. "Sure," he said. "I'm on my way out. Lock up when you leave, okay?"

Nate hustled out the door, violin case in hand, and Abby sat on the couch and dialed the house in Barnegat Point.

Adele's excited voice came on the line. "Hello?"

"Happy birthday!" Abby cried.

"Abby! I'm ten today! I have two numbers in my age!"

Abby laughed. "Did you get my package?"

"It came yesterday, but Helen made me wait until this morning to open it. Thank you for the doll."

"I got her for you in Chinatown. Her dress is made of real silk."

"She's the best doll in my whole collection."

Abby listened to Adele's chatter and then said hello to Pop and to Helen. When she had hung up the phone, she pulled Nate's spare key out of her purse, locked his door, and continued upstairs to her apartment.

She opened the door, turned on the light, and wished she had a cat. Something friendly and warm to greet her at the end of the day. She hung her coat on the rack and took the pork chop into the tiny kitchen. Abby had lived in this apartment for almost two years and still couldn't quite believe how small the kitchen was.

The pork chop was sizzling in a pan and Abby was listening to the news on the radio when her doorbell rang. Abby scowled. Mrs. Graumann had a habit of showing up just as she was getting ready to eat. Abby flung open the door, preparing to tell Mrs. Graumann that she had only one pork chop.

Zander Burley stood before her. He was holding a dozen red roses.

He looked exactly the same, and exactly different. Abby felt as if one second had passed, not five years, and she was standing in the Burleys' parlor in the fading light, watching Zander's face crumple.

Zander held out the roses. "Happy Valentine's Day," he said. "Will you marry me?"

Acknowledgments

This book, which I approached with some trepidation, since it was my first foray into writing about an era that was before my time, would not have taken shape without the help of a number of people who generously shared their time and talents with me, both when the story was in its infancy, and at later stages as it unfolded. Noa Wheeler, my intrepid researcher, was a marvel at problem solving, and at finding creative ways to address my many, many ... many questions. From locating people for interviews to sussing out obscure articles, she allowed me to give depth, color, and detail to the characters and the setting.

Special thanks to Betty Knight, who was twice interviewed by Noa, and who painted a fascinating picture of her childhood. Born in 1926, she grew up in a rural Maine community, and she patiently answered our endless questions about everything from iceboxes to wallpaper to working women.

Thanks, too, to Professor Stephen Murphy at the University of Southern Maine for his help with our queries about schooling for Abby's brother Fred.

Several people in my own family, all long gone by the time I began working on Family Tree, nevertheless inspired the story in their own ways. From my great-aunt Grace I inherited three cartons of memorabilia and family papers, including her copy of *My School Days Memory Book*, in which I found many details for Abby's *Commencement Days* book and her high school graduation.

In 1918 my great-grandfather sent his daughter Adele, my grandmother, a three-page letter that has now become famous in our family. In it, he counseled Adele, whose fiancé (my grandfather Lyman Martin) had just proposed to her, to wait to get married until after Lyman had finished his service in World War I and was in a better position to provide for her. "Why not act in this matter just as both of you have acted up to this point," my great-grandfather wrote, "with reason, and regard for propriety?" But my grandmother was as headstrong as Abby Nichols proved to be when Luther counseled her to marry Zander. Abby turned down Zander's proposal, and my grandparents got married almost immediately, while my grandfather was on a three-day pass from the army. (And they lived happily ever after.)

Finally, many thanks to my editor, David Levithan; my

agent, Amy Berkower; and Ellie Berger, Charisse Meloto, Lizette Serrano, Rachel Coun, and the team at Scholastic.

I'm deeply grateful to everyone who played a part in the story of Abigail Cora Nichols.

Thank you.

About the Author

Ann M. Martin in the acclaimed and bestselling author of a number of novels and series, including *Belle Teal*, *A Corner of the Universe* (a Newbery Honor book), *A Dog's Life*, *Here Today*, *P.S. Longer Letter Later* (written with Paula Danziger), the Doll People series (written with Laura Godwin), the Main Street series, and the generation-defining series The Baby-sitters Club. She lives in New York.